THE AGE OF CLADAN

Jim Bell

ISBN: 978-0-6480946-0-9

www.jbellstories.com

At ten man is an animal
At twenty a lunatic
At thirty a failure
At forty a fraud
And at fifty a criminal

Author unknown

CONTENTS

THE AGE OF
CLADAN

PART ONE

9
THE DEAD ALTAR BOY COMEDIAN

When Cladan was little he and his older sister Haley were whisked off to hospital with a bug at the same time, but only Cladan came home in the end; sans a gland and bloated on ice cream. It was two weeks later when Haley died and Cladan wondered if his little brother Haxt or his oldest sister Sunnie had ever seen her eat any of the *"tiny red apples"* hanging off the tree by the gate.

"Never!" they swore.

They'd all long been warned not to ever near the *Cotoneaster*. Or maybe she'd chewed on a leaf from the old black maple bleeding sap by the porch, which no one could bear — it was like a running sore. The three of them couldn't work out which tree was the more to blame.

Theories were rife and coming from everyone to explain her suddenly gone. Half the neighbours wondered if it had more to do with their pop's penchant for the underworld; an array of shrunken heads from his travels were long displayed across the sill of the lounge room window, their stitched-up lips and eyelids scaring off the locals and birds. To top it all off, on the night of her burial, the tall poplar tree in the front yard suddenly fell over onto the roof of the house and emergency services were called out to pick it off with a crane. After that, everyone in the street forever deemed the place cursed. Kids pointed it out in passing like it was the local haunted house.

"Don't gawk," some would say, *"they can steal a face and craft a doll!"*

So the family soon shifted away from the cracked earth street of their ma's few estranged kin — their pop had none, being a bastard war orphan from Gibraltar — to the other side of town to run a cafe by the shores of Flip Bay.

Over time, Cladan and his brother and sister had built a dozen spaceships out of drink crates in the tiny backyard of the store. He'd strap a Schweppes crate to his back like it was a jet pack and roam the skies beneath the boughs.

"Will? ... Will? ... Will? ..."

"Penny? ... Penny? ... Penny? ..."

Only weak shards of daylight could ever shimmer through the branches of the giant oak in the corner of the yard that hung wide and heavy across the lot like a talon; reaching over the little backyards of the butcher's next door, the grocer's next to that, and the toy shop's and the dentist's on the other side. It was the only tree on the block they'd never climbed, because of the cicadas, which terrified them, as they always wailed in a choir of thousands. At dusk, deafening mobs of them sometimes huddled by the back step, blaring in the streaky moonlight. Then sometimes at dawn all that'd be left would be a dead gutted silence and a dozen brown corpse shells clinging to the back door, crunchy as cornflakes. Cladan would only pick one off and it'd just crumble in his little hand to atoms. Late one night he wouldn't walk past the tree to get to the outer because of them all, so he unloaded on the pathway, where he prayed their junkie pop would skid on in the morning and lynch himself in a web long spun for years to catch the greens. None of them liked the insects there — they were the size of dogs.

Come twilight, their ma would shut up the store for the day and their pop would lay out his *"pixie pills"* across the kitchen sink for the night and swill them all down with lemonade as the evening passed.

"That 'cken lie is not a laugh. And this life is not a canker. Take that guff back and save the salt!"

At some point he'd vanish out into the pitch-black store and stagger back into the light with a horde of sweets in his skinny arms and slouch back under the sunlamp, staring at the TV above the fridge, slurring Esperanto, and just gorge away, never offering his kids a crumb.

"Kies kokido? Kiun vojon?"

Cladan, with his only brother, his only sister ever foreseeable, sat dutifully for three years behind the kitchen table, watching their pop run past to and fro as he beat their ma with the pans.

"La Butiko devas fari monon!"

At his new school Cladan had the chance to become one of the Three Wise Men in a nativity play, and his pop made him a large treasure chest out of cardboard, painting it a deep aqua, with blotches and sparkles all over it, so it looked old and rusty, and covered with the remnant scabs of deep-sea barnacles. Cladan wanted to fill it with some of his toys, as gifts to be bestowed upon the baby Lord, but he only wound up a simple shepherd in the end. His pop soon made him a staff instead, with a large white hook to round his flock, but it was flexible wire and all of his sheep passed through.

But Cladan loved his new school and soon grew obsessed with science and evolution; igneous rocks and prehistoric mammals; reptiles and amphibians; the dugong and the tapir; the lamprey and the sloth. Burma too, held a similar fascination; the langur and the mouse deer; the invincible lungfish of the Irrawaddy.

Our Immanuel of the Most Precious Blood was split into two distinct worlds: dirt and grass to the boys, asphalt and concrete to the girls. No one ever trespassed. Though Cladan had an unofficial sweetheart of some daring: Amber Greely, who was a tomboy at heart.

"I can climb that gum quicker than you," she'd tease him on the way home from school, and suddenly they'd be heading to the sky.

Though, to the surprise of her friends, sometimes she'd stand obsessed at the borderline between the grounds, looking out for him playing somewhere on the busy oval, and she'd hang over the edge with her nose, waiting for it to be pecked, recess after recess. Sometimes she'd stay there whole lunchtimes till he'd come to her.

"Mmm-wha," he'd say in passing, pecking her nose with a kiss, and was gone again, chasing a ball with his mates.

Then, other times, when he never appeared, she'd swing out on a long imaginary vine, calling out for him as she'd slowly swing back, always conscious that the invisible vine was the only magic, and that any action without it would've pushed the nearest snitch to a monitor, followed by a caning by the nuns.

Sometimes after school Cladan would belt the drums around for a while with his friends out in the middle of the oval, trying to outwit one another.

"Neil Armstrong was the first meat on the moon!"

"Pianos are made out of elephants and trees!"

Then they'd head off to his parents' cafe for sausage rolls, which they'd sandwich in all the crusts left over from the loaves the locals swallowed. Though Cladan would eat his in a roll, proclaiming all the while, *"The Sausage Roll Roll"* his only patent...

Come the new year a nun suddenly realized that Cladan was of age to serve, and before he knew it he was soon swinging burning myrrh by the local dead each morning without amiss.

"Your funeral!" his ma, Elli, would rasp, shaking him awake at dawn, hacking on her third Salem. Then she'd swish back along the hallway in her bubbly dressing gown and clamber down the stairs to greet the store's first delivery, maligning the world.

"The dead dropped at every dawn."

Over time Cladan was soon promoted from the funerals at dawn to his first Sunday Mass; but none of the other altar boys turned up, and he knew of no moves to make or how to assist the priest in the slightest.

He'd only ever seen one Mass on the Sabbath in his whole eight years, as no one in his family had stepped inside a church since Haley had died: his ma had given up on God, and that was four years ago.

"An Indian-giver to the enth," she'd scoff.

All he knew to do was what the old Scottish priest hiccupped to him in the vestry before the Mass.

"Come sacring... the soundings are to occur thricely over the course of the dirge... in gradual increments... and of equal passage."

But their cues were a complete mystery to him, and he was terrified, kneeling there alone in his red and white robes before the crowd, that God might simply annihilate him on the spot in front of everyone — as an example — if he got the timing of even one of them wrong.

If He can take Haley for nothing . . .

Then he sensed a moment of import — the way they all rose to their feet as one — so he rang hard and loud. But the priest darted a look back at him through his thick bottle-lens like he'd just cut his thumb.

I'm gone.

And he tried to stifle the mixed tones still hanging on the air, but he fumbled on his knees and fell over to one side, tangling his robes, clanging the chimes all about as he knelt back up again — his face stricken with terror — as he finally crouched down low and engulfed them all to silence like he was smothering a crab.

I'm dead as done.

But the congregation suddenly burst out laughing. Then seconds later flipped back to silence just as quickly again, with everyone squirming in the pews, trying to stifle themselves — nostrils hissing about like snakes everywhere — like nothing had happened.

As the old priest resumed the mass, Cladan could feel himself blushing so hard he thought he might simply dissolve into the blood-red carpet at his knees like it was the blotting paper of Hell just waiting to soak him up for the slightest glitch, before finally being tossed back into the ether again, where he might only have the slimmest chance of ever being gambled on again, as say a gnat, or if he was lucky, a thrip.

Then he gradually took a look out the corners of his eyes, only to find the congregation not glued to the priest up in the pulpit, but slyly at him; all of them smiling in the stained-glass sunshine and candlelight.

Everyone suddenly looked so friendly, he thought. Then he nervously smiled back at them all, like he was trying to make amends for the error.

But they'd always look away, biting on their lips again.

And whenever he looked back and didn't smile, and just looked on at them in thought, trying to comprehend it all, some of them covered their mouths with their hands, and pinched their noses, with their eyes bulged out like balloons, just in case they might start up another roar across the rafters.

And, as a scientist, Cladan would look to this assortment of blue faces starved for air everywhere, scattered wide across a sea of silent grins, with wonder.

It was like spotting an algal bloom; a phenomenon rarely witnessed at ignition.

But he'd never heard such open laughter like that before; certainly never back home in the sullen confines of the family store.

It was a shock to him.

People can be suddenly free, when they choose to be, at the drop of a hat.

And he looked away from them all and thought about the whole puzzling notion of misery everyone was sourly locked into for the hour, and the odd way everyone sheepishly swallowed the slightest morsel of happiness they'd all ever shared as one together; only to instantly resume the gloom all over again.

It's too easy not to laugh.

He'd long been wondering why, at his age, right after losing Haley, he'd had to stand in front of coffins every morning anyway. And now, on the official day of rest, to have to swallow yet more sorrow all over again. Couldn't he just have fun like every other kid out in the sun?

Why is this my life?

Why did he have to deal with death all the time? Burying the dead every dawn, and now drinking blood and eating human flesh, with a giant ragged man nailed to the wall everywhere he turned.

How does all that work? he wondered. *How does the letting of blood save everyone?*

No one had ever properly explained the details to him.

Is blood a currency? A tool to barter?

The whole thing baffled him in the end, and growing bored, with his knees aching from kneeling on the spot for so long, he soon decided to ring every now and again, when the priest would least expect it, just to see what would happen if everyone was happy again.

When that old lady's face opens up she looks half her age.

Sometimes letting loose one long relentless clang kept everyone beaming for minutes. And soon, he didn't feel so scared of God anymore, for letting him help people feel less troubled. He was aiming for tears of joy, instead of all those rivers of grief he'd watched spill every dawn. So he kept on ringing every few minutes, just to keep everyone cheery; watching all the sad old faces finally opening up to who they each really were inside, without fear of blackmail of what might happen to them when, one day, they'd be dead too, just like Jesus nailed to the wall.

After the Mass was over, Cladan wasn't punished for his antics at all. In consideration for being such a young novice, and that he was the only one left to perform the rituals of six seniors, his mistakes were immediately forgiven and he was duly sent on his way home as if nothing had happened. That bright Sunday noon Cladan headed home convinced he was a comedian with the blessing of Christ...

Another schizo Melbourne winter soon rolled around and Cladan's ninth birthday was coming up. His brother Haxt knew what the family were getting for him; and Haxt knew that Cladan knew that he knew all that; and Cladan knew that Haxt knew all that as well, etc. One dead Sunday afternoon while they were both outside playing amongst the shut-up shops, Cladan stopped at the toy shop window and started pointing out toys he'd long desired in passing, asking if his gift would be this or that, using the Bible as his truth serum — he'd seen it used a hundred times in the dock on *Consider Your Verdict* without it ever once failing.

"The Batman utility belt."

"No."

"Swear on the Holy Bible?"

"Yep."

His eyes took to a microscope with a collapsible mainframe that folded the whole thing up into a double-barreled pistol from another world, called an Opal Lobster.

"Is that it?"

"Nup," snapped Haxt.

"Swear on the Holy Bible?"

"Yep."

He pointed out a plastic Gila monster that could be disassembled down through each biological system to its bones, complete with venom tracts, refillable poison sacs, and a jaw that could crush ice to splinters; a 1:6 scale B-9, Class M-3 General Utility Non-Theorizing Environmental Control Robot; a Junior Chemistry Lab Set with fool's plutonium and eruptible volcano; till soon he was pointing out the more tackier items he didn't really want across the floor of the display.

Then he spotted it, on its back, under a layer of dust in a corner of the window, which he thought he'd long missed out on and would never see on show again, and he gestured to it.

"That?"

Haxt shook his head, looking away.

"*Swear on the Holy Bible?*" Cladan thundered. "*The fulcrum of life!*"

But Haxt dropped his eyes, and lowered his head, looking strangely hangdog, then sheepishly doled out a soft but reluctant, "*Nup*" as he looked away again.

Cladan found out! He was finally getting the rare commemorative yoyo of the last great space catastrophe! He was so happy that day!

Though, all that was sorted later on; when he went upstairs to their room and flicked on the light — only to find himself thrashing about the doorjamb to a sudden blackout. As payback for being spiritually blackmailed, Haxt had unscrewed the light-switch cover so Cladan poked his fingers in the wires. All Cladan could hear as he flipped about the floor was a rankled little laugh of comeuppance from the shadows. Which, later, on reflection, he stoically took on the chin out of guilt — as a just riposte for such a mortal sin as religious extortion — and swayed by conscience promptly dropped all dreams of ever remaining a heretical comic.

And though one day, weeks later, Cladan nudged Haxt to follow suit as they crossed the road as usual, Haxt suddenly hesitated out of mistrust, then reconsidered, and was bowled over by a cab right outside the cafe door — but he just bounced down the road like a ball and got through it with just a scratch like Cladan.

It seemed like half the family had turned on each other since Haley's passing. Except for Sunnie, who studied hard for school and played her 45s with friends over and over as the only way to help blot out missing her roommate and confidante.

One morning out in the playground everyone watched Rory swing high on the swings the way the nuns had long forbid, and everyone soon saw why. He swung himself so high that he circled the bar several times, accelerating with every revolution, till suddenly he ended up tangled at the top like a bow-tie: hands, knees, elbows, and shoes poking out every which way, in a taut little knot of himself. Some students in the context of their religious instruction saw catechistic parallels and instinctively knelt, crossing themselves in prayer. That same day, giant-jawed Jarvis slipped off the monkey bars after a daring five-bar lunge, and fell to the ground, exposing the bones of his elbows and knees clear as day. All these strange accidents were starting to unfold everywhere.

It was around this time someone in the middle of the night splashed *"JC WAS THE FIRST SOCIALIST"* in tall white letters with a house brush across the rounded end of the wall surrounding the school, so the peak-hour traffic would see it as they circled the roundabout and passed the church and mansions to head out into bayside. And that's where Cladan first saw Sibyl up close: a mad old frowsy local in a red hat and rags who always shook her cane in the air and screamed an indecipherable barrage of venom at all the kids after school.

One day, as Cladan rushed out to head home, he almost crashed into her, and froze on seeing her up close, as she gave him the eye and roared down at him.

"Huthagellothago!"

And he scrambled across the road, through the middle of the roundabout, and drudged home along the train tracks, where the tall fennel shoots towered everywhere like trees and reeked like the piss of a hemorrhaging animal. Sybil was regarded as an all-too-real flesh-and-blood monster on the loose, and no kid could ever understand why she went about on a daily rampage like that, terrifying everyone all the time. Cladan made up a twisted gargoyle face to mimic her, which soon spread across the school grounds, but was suddenly banned by the teachers and nuns for its unnerving look.

Parents grew concerned when their kids were pulling the face at home, ringing the school...

"Our kids look like the Hunchbacks of Notre Dame!"

But all it took was a simple word of warning about what would happen if the wind ever changed; which convinced every kid to drop it, because no one ever wanted to end up looking like Sybil for good and being forever reviled by everyone as just a pest.

Gradually the two worlds of school oversteered their orbits and a rumour started circulating about a secret after-school party coming up, but no one could ever find out any more about it. Cladan first heard of it when they were playing the drums after hours out in the oval.

"Whose birthday is it then?"

"No one's saying!"

A few days later Cladan started walking Amber home with his best friend, Remy, who was shyly walking home Amber's best friend, Shari, who lived directly opposite the old iron school gates. (It was always a frustrated walk for Remy, never being able to talk with Shari as much as he longed to in the space of just 50 steps.) Then a kombi screeched to a stop on the crossing, and the side door slid open, revealing a tight inner universe of screaming girls. Amber and Shari shoved Cladan and Remy inside, and leapt in too, sliding the door shut behind them, and the kombi roared away with Amber's mother driving like a maniac, laughing her head off.

At Amber's birthday party, they all span the bottle. Cladan and Remy were the only boys there, and were getting pecked kisses galore from everyone. Though Amber only allowed her friends to peck Cladan on the forehead, and Cladan could only kiss their hands like an old-time suitor, except with red-haired Marla, who everyone ruled out kissing either boy because she had ringworms.

Then one sunny day, months later, after a screaming fight in the quadrangle with all the other girls, Marla snitched to a nun about that old summer party when they span the bottle, which instigated a thorough school inquiry. The teachers and nuns interrogated every student from the party as if they were all devils incarnate — particularly Remy and Cladan.

"Did anyone leap to a kiss?"

"In what manner had there been subservience?"

"Did any lay with another?"

"Was there a goad of any kind?"

"By which impudent mind so purged of light could this be offered?"

"And by which heart so blinded could this be sought?"

"The evil that resides in a touch can bring about the fall of man!"

Cladan and Remy, and Amber and Shari, and the rest of the girls from class were all shocked by this: their young inner eyes finally opened up to the general inherent rottenness of people, all along vaguely and mysteriously alluded to, which their dedicated tutors had ironically long strived to never let happen.

Soon, Cladan was no longer interested in rocks and minerals, or The Animal Kingdom, or Burma anymore. Within weeks he left that stretch of the bay with what was left of his family, to hastily merge with the dilapidated half of another in ruins, a few shires up — sans their doped-out pop, left behind to rot in the store with all the paling chocolates. Though Cladan didn't tell Amber he was leaving. He only told Remy at the last minute on the way home from school, on his final day there, when parting near their homes as usual, and they both stopped in the street and sat on a brick fence in the sunshine and cried together.

Cladan instantly had a larger family, and they were all suddenly poor, living in a fibro shack without power, cooking on a kerosene heater, and sharing stinking beds together. One day two new offsiders in the pack took Cladan out fishing, where with a crowd of locals they all saw a manta ray circling in the shallows. And everyone rushed to the other side of the pier to watch it slowly glide out from under them all and flap its way free back out to sea.

"*Oh, he's lost,*" everyone kept saying. "*He's completely lost.*"

Then later, just like the nuns had warned, both of them hooked Cladan to one side like a sleepy carp, under the sway of sniffing glue by the squeaky tea trees of a secluded lagoon, where one night, weeks later, after more of it, he walked off into the sea, out past the sandbars, and tried to end himself.

And in a blur, out of the blue, Haxt suddenly requested to stay with an aunt and uncle for a while, and never returned. And Sunnie visited cousins as well, and stayed the same. And Cladan never knew why they'd gone, or why someone didn't pluck him out as well. He was just left to the fog that had suddenly enveloped him, filtering out anything that'd ever made sense to him.

Of those times all he'd ever recall in later life was him sitting alone on the roof of the house one dusk, throwing down pine cones at the pair sniffing petrol from the rusted-out bomb on the front lawn; both of them laughing it up, and staggering around like loons, as they threw all the knives and forks from the kitchen drawer at the sad old black horse Star cowering in the corner of the empty lot next door.

Though Cladan didn't know it, it was all soon found out in the end, and the pair suddenly fled to the other side of town and back into the arms of their loins like worms. And Cladan never knew why they'd both suddenly gone, either, or what had ever really happened to him. He even thought he missed them, and was crying for that all along. He heard some of them ran away in the years to come. And some soon died. And others became highly anaesthetized. Sometimes a clock spring just unwinds and scatters time like the stars...

14
DOWN TO THE MOONS

In the city there was never enough sand to fall. Cladan was leaning on his elbows in the tiny wooden office of Gasal's Car Parking Emporium, watching the little pile rise in the hourglass again. Then he upended it, and watched it begin to slowly tower all over again. The same way Gasal would during the day, and all the other students on shifts would do as well. There was just nothing else to do. But on a Friday night, after a long dull day at school, time would seem to crawl. Little to know, till midnight, when returning on the last train home, that during one of those spells when the grains had spun a dream, Gasal was burning to death.

Around twilight, his melancholy ma, Elli — who slept alone in her own room — was roused by a fireman in mask, her room ablaze. But by the time she was helped out the window, and slid down the chute to the ground, it was too late for them to return to fetch Gasal. High flames were already licking past the sill of his room and snapping out at the cold night air. Elli just stood helplessly below on the front lawn, shouting up to him, as she often did from the lounge at the oddest hours to coax him out.

"Gasal! Wake up! A good movie's on! Gas! Cool Hand Luke's on!"

But her soused de facto spouse slept more soundly than she, and would not be moved till he was a cindered corpse.

It was around this time, the skirmishes began — an eruption long heralded by the bankers at large ever since the umpteenth rise in rates the year before. Whispered behind hands, they called it *"The Morrow War"*: it was bound to come. All the locals were already more than armed with secret caches of clubs planted about the gardens of town. And the looting soon began, and within days the sky was so blackened from all the fires that it was hard going for any to tell when real night began: the moon seemed forever gone, with all the stars clammed, and all the nervous birdsong trapped beneath the fug. People were going mad everywhere from the racket of all the dogs: the maddened ants fleeing the fires were swarming all over them for quicker getaways, sending them all yelping wild into the creeks and ponds. Most pups ended up simply drowning themselves in the bay just to get away from the itch.

Gasal had not even been buried yet when one night in a freezing storm more looters struck. At dawn Cladan and his ma arrived at the chapel to send Gasal off to the beyond, only to find the vicar gone, all the pews ripped out of the floor, the chapel barren as a barn, but for Gasal in a zoot suit on the marble altar — robbed of his casket for fuel — with his charred hands still crossed on his chest, and the rats already through his boots to his toes. But still solemn to the occasion afforded them — and not unsadly, but ungodly — they both gently lifted him and carried him down the highway, little caring of the blasts careening about them.

Out on the open road they bumped into Heather, the old blind war doctor who lived in the flat beneath them, tapping her cane along the gradient. She'd been a tenant there for years and it seemed they could never be free of her. She would often tap her cane up against the ceiling to be told the time, and Cladan would read the clock on the lounge room wall and stamp flatfootedly the hour in quick succession, then slowly strum the heater bars like a harp the proxing minutes. Though, for the last year or two, he'd make up the time just to shut her up. Usually a good few extra stamps on the floor with both feet would send her off to bed early and give them all some welcome peace for the night. But then she'd end up tapping up at dawn again, not yet hearing the birds, thinking she'd missed it and slept in again. But out on the highway, carrying their load, they didn't see her at first — she'd sought them out by the scent of Elli's beloved. Perhaps Heather had known Gasal more intimately, Elli sometimes thought, as she'd often pondered since he'd taken separate quarters because of his snores.

Cladan was surprised to see her out, what with all the fireworks going off, but she said she found it all quite musical.

"Ah, the pure resonance of detonations," — a guilty pleasure she developed in the war as a WAC she couldn't seem to shake. Then she drifted off into her old diatribe of *"tonal harmonics"*, and without amiss, as she always did, she brought up the dear subject of Bach again. But she helped them both with Gasal,

taking a leg from Elli, and they continued on towards the infirmary as she calmly hummed songs to the artillery — the triggery of the catapults loading at their sides; the nails hailing down across the corrugated roofs about them. She'd seen many a corpse, she said, in the good ol' days when she could see, and that was enough. And as for the smell, it had never left her palate.

"Once the olfactory's got that one in, the rest is purely cheese."

They didn't carry Gasal across the park as planned — the footbridge having been cut over the ravine — so they returned home. But once they reached the front gate, they laid him down by the letterbox for a rest in the sun, and Heather, kneeling inquisitively at his side, brushing one of her curious cats away, partly undressed Gasal and felt the charred irregularities of his features, mumbling softly to herself — as if back under mask — the various Latin regions of his carcass. There was a strange sort of beauty about it, this blind surgeon examining the remains of one of God's own, thought both ma and son, dumbly watching on. It seemed natural. But soon, Heather felt sickened by her callous nostalgia, and suddenly re·covered him.

Subtly looking at his ma, Cladan pondered at how grief seemed the most unpredictable of emotions; how it not only seemed to belie a frighteningly subjective logic all its own, but longed to be absolved through the rite of openly expressing it, like every other emotion. For some, stricken by grief, Cladan wondered at how they'd often mourn in darkness all their long lonely lives; and others, only to their creeping anniversaries. And how many of the dead lay honoured in granite with frequent flowers; then all the others, only to be so grandly tucked in and eternally forgotten. To Cladan, what ran through the bereaved mind of his ma when she did what she did, he could only ever attribute to the nagging volatility of her inherited Mexican corpuscles — though Elli had never set foot there in the old homeland of her kin. All she'd ever breathed her whole life long was the crispy southern air of Australia. But Cladan often wondered how much of all that Old World blood not shed by the Inquisitors had his grandma duly passed on to her daughter, and on to himself. There were other triggers too, aside from his ancestry, Cladan thought, which could have initiated the strange urge to which suddenly his ma grievously succumbed...

As a curious teenage girl growing up in the bush of Leongatha Elli often frequented the local rubbish dump with her friends. Over one long weekend of rummaging amongst the high mounds of trash, she once assembled from all her finds a total bicycle, complete with a strange rear wheel with a massive inner hub, which, when pedaled back a turn, magically changed its ratio. Other discarded articles Elli discovered there, which more than once kept her and her family preoccupied, were an assortment of bird cages for their pet budgerigars, which they all linked together as one vast snaking aviary of twisted bends wrapped around the entire perimeter of their property. Elli reasoned that, though cruel as it was that the birds were still caged, they were at least granted a much more variable freedom than those imprisoned in pet stores, which enabled them all to swiftly and gracefully glide through their own private universe, and often at great speeds, sometimes racing one another around the house for hours.

One strange day at the dump, Elli prodded a large plastic bag in the garbage, and out fell a severed baby's leg, with assorted entrails. The police soon uncovered a dozen human waste disposal bags containing everything from amputated limbs to discarded gizzards, aborted fetuses, and great glowing husks of cancer the size of watermelons, all of which rocked the state government for its penny-thieving health practices. And it was on that day, the last Elli ever sifted through the muckheap, that she found a discarded dummy that would bring her own ma back to life.

Elli's ma, Seresi Serosa, a proud yet overwhelmingly sad marketer in town, long dispirited by homesickness for the Yucatan of her youth, dourly returned home that evening, and it was only when she arrived at the gate to check the mail — and she'd long said this to all her peers back at the stalls till her dying day — that it was only then that she found herself truly home. Standing tall at the front gate, up to its knees in weeds, stood a black shop mannequin, painted with the luminous bones of its skeleton, and with her home's letterbox nailed between its blades as its head and crowning glory. Tears welled in her eyes on just seeing it, as it brought back so many glorious memories of her youth in Valladolid; all those colourful parades of the November dead she'd witnessed with astonishment as a girl, with all the huge paper mache figures of the spirit world dancing about everywhere, and the millions of stalls with stacked sugar skulls in her own name and those of her family and friends, and how everyone would just squat down in the packed gutters of the streets to eat their own heads, thickly smeared with ice cream and raspberry topping, and watch the procession sweep along, laughing their guts out.

Seresi was soon so overwhelmed with flooding memories and emotions that she had to lean on the fence to contain herself, and like an old cactus of her homeland, slowly, she found herself squeezing out the old joyous tears of her childhood, one by one, till she was born again.

And when she looked up at the breadth of her home, with a sudden new regard for what she now had, she saw through her flooding eyes, her little girl, Elli, at the 2nd floor window, leaning on her elbows on the sill, watching down at her with a pleased smile. And she smiled back in tears herself, and like she told everyone at the stalls, she saw her own ma looking down at what she'd done for her, and her grandma and what she'd done for her, and the whole ghost stock cast of her proud ancestry in approval.

And for that whole night, her ma sat out there on the fence, under the stars, with Elli at one side, and her beautifully gruesome letterbox at the other, guzzling mezcal for the first time in a long while, giving her daughter her first worm, as her own ma had done, and her ma had done, and for the first time in 20 years, since migrating, she rediscovered her own private Mexico and felt complete again...

So perhaps only Cladan could ever understand what his ma did that day — for Elli was his ma, and his ma was him, and that was the Yucatan and all those roads within, and what that meant to Cladan would be more important to him than what anyone would ever think.

Elli began to rock loose her letterbox post outside the block of flats, and when she'd plucked it out, she began to use it as a pick to widen the hole, and she scooped all the dirt out with her hands, making it longer and deeper till the tiny garden was an open grave, and she laid her de facto love down inside it and began to bury him. Then, after she gently patted down the last of the soil, she returned the post back to its place, by the head of Gasal; the letterbox bearing their new family name. For she reasoned, what better site could there be for his place of rest than at the door of his only grieving kin? Gasal would be the first to receive the best sent wishes of birthdays and the sacred cheers of Christmas to pass on blessed to his final love, and her son, whom Gasal had pretty much regarded his own. It would be doubly fitting, Elli thought, as the family headstone, where, one by one, she and her son would surely go. It seemed more reasonable an address to spend eternity's days than amongst a million loveless pastures of abandoned stones.

Cladan and his ma never did ascend the stairs again to their gutted home. They soon wormed themselves in with the old blind doctor and her cats. And Heather could cook quite well as she'd whistle Johannes's fugues, and she didn't ever have to raise her stick to the sky anymore to know the time — it was just a matter of asking. And each day by their door, there were always the brightest flowers there blooming fresh for Gasal. Though secretively, Elli still often entertained the whim of exhuming him one night and wrapping him up as a mummy, and painting him black like the old dummy she once found for her ma, then propping him up at the gate as a letterbox, with his even pearly whites just slightly ajar to clutch the bills. Though Elli never did get to

Mexico like she'd long promised her ma she would. But now, like her ma, she felt as if she finally had it with her instead — like a great clump of its magical dirt forever clutched in her fist to her dying step.

And Cladan would be back at the lot on Monday morning, with no more school, staring at the tumbler again, flipping it over and over, watching every grain drop down again through the void, nibbling his nails down to the moons.

16
NEVER MORE DELUDED
BY A HAPPINESS

The hotel room was even more dingy than Cladan had imagined it would be, and he felt a little embarrassed on just stepping inside, and wondered if he'd done the wrong thing in choosing it. All the old glue was browning through the wallpaper everywhere, and the bathroom was falling apart in crumbs from the ceiling down. Clearly, the residue of blood had faintly stained the towels, and the soap was as small as a coin, and as used, with little fat fingerprints all over the trademark. But he was nervous, and in a hurry, and he stepped reluctantly under the rickety shower — the hot water piercing through him like wires. Then he dried himself off with toilet paper, trying to see his hair in the old foggy mirror, whilst out in the lounge, a mouse was already nibbling at his laces like they were linguine.

Through an open window, he stopped and listened to a lady either badly singing or brilliantly screaming as he dressed: he wasn't sure. Then a dog soon howled in accompaniment from somewhere, and a madman laughed out in the corridor. But a little girl, crying floors above on a landing, was louder than everyone, the traffic below, just everything: softly weeping, but loud. The whole place echoing like an asylum. Then a bug scuttled across his bare toes and he lashed out at it impulsively, stamping it dead with his foot. With blood and mush smeared across his sole, he dunked it back under the shower, but this time cold.

As the sun slowly slipped away, rainbow lights flashed into the room and fell across the skinny bed as violent winds swished past the window like the ocean, weaving through the tall buildings, composing little tunes that Cladan hummed to, as he swigged on his cider and stared out across the city lights. He picked up the phone just to make sure it was working. Maybe she wouldn't ring first after all, he thought. He thought about how he'd met her in a queue that afternoon, waiting to get a tram ticket as well. He could see her clearly in his mind, and the way she tapped her foot, and for a moment he wondered if there was music going on when she did that, which he didn't hear or pay attention to, when she suddenly asked him where he lived, and he blurted out he was from interstate, and just passing through, and he blindly threw the name of the old hotel at her, out of the blue.

Then the dog howled again, and a drunk ferociously yelled out, *"Kill me now!"* from a window in the old dosshouse next door — the words echoing up the lane, and up the side of the old hotel, swooping into the room like a bat.

Increasingly anxious, he opened the door a little, just in case she came early. Then after a while he started to look down the hall for her. An old man with a giant fuzzy hat on was standing at the elevator door, staring up at the numbers. Cladan went back inside and ate the last complimentary biscuit, then peeped back out, but the man was still there, staring up. So he went over to the window again and stared out across the city, and looked down into the busy street where everything just groaned pain and proud of it; people ambling everywhere like ants; cars honking all over the road; lights flashing all over the place. Bored, and getting drunker, he dribbled out of the window, but he was too high up to know if he ever hit anyone. He had a smoke and dropped the butt down too, but heard nothing, not a scream. Then he grabbed the bottle and took another deep swig, and poured a spurt outside just for the hell of it, imagining some old wino on the path below — head back, throat open, catching every drip leaked from the heavens.

He yelled across the rooftops, *"Kiss me now!"* for the hell of it, but no one answered. Everything just continued as normal. No reply.

But the lights across the road at the rooftop ice-rink gave off great colours as the sun vanished in the distance across the bay. His chin felt warmer. Then he drained the bottle, and dropped it out the window as well — still hearing nothing, not even the smash he knew was there. It was like a bottomless well, and he suddenly wished he had an old fishing rod with him — the old cane one he once fished up from the end of a pier when he was a kid, complete with a fancy reel that still turned and an old rusty lure that still managed to swivel like it'd just been granted a second life.

"Someone just spat on me!"

Cladan turned around, and there she was, standing in the door jam, glistening in the light of a 40-watt globe, wearing a red frilly dress she knew he'd like. Her hair was as white as her skin and her skin was as luminous as a dove's. Her eyes were the shape of boats, with the rich interswirled colours of coral. Then she waddled over on her fat heels and kissed him on both cheeks, and held onto him tight. She was glad to see him, he could tell. Then she sat down on the bed with him as he shyly looked off, mentioning it was his first time, and then he asked her how much . . .

17

HIS CAREER AS A HOLE

Cladan stepped off Mr. Fylfot's grave with an idling chainsaw in his hand, wiping sweat away from his eyes, catching his breath. His knuckles were bloodied under the ratty gloves, and blisters had already begun to burst open in huge bubbles across his palms.

THENAR FYLFOT
BORN 1833
BELOVED HUSBAND OF A FEW
DEVOTED FATHER OF MANY
DIED 1908

Two weeks earlier the sky fell in a little during a storm and cut through Melbourne like a skinning knife. In the middle of a cemetery not far from Cladan's bedsit a giant oak centuries old was severed at the roots and lay toppled over rows of long forgotten vaults. Cladan had spotted it from the street and applied for a job there for the week to help pay the rent.

He stood there, hatted and goggled, his watch ticking on Ms. Kildecat's shrine, with all day to go.

The branches never seemed to end.

He imagined the cloud of Hiroshima frozen into this singular husk, stretched over hundreds of tombs in every direction, reburying the dead all over again.

He cut at the limbs all morning, standing on pillars and gates and plaques, all long untouched and sacred. Some of the greediest branches had grown through crypts, and many of the huge roots had tunneled deep into mausoleums like straws into malted-milks.

When he'd cut a large spread of the boughs away he threw them all into an old cart — once a hearse in the old horse and buggy days — and jumped down on them all to cram in more and more. Then, like a dutiful Clydesdale, he slowly dragged it down the winding path on its half-flat tyres through the fields of stones and emptied it all out behind the office for a giant bonfire at the end of the week. Neil and Barry were looking forward to lighting it all up.

It was only three days since Melbourne's second homicidal rampage in a fortnight, and 10 days before Christmas.

Neil, the foreman of the few young diggers, told Cladan to fill in a grave at noon.

"Go up to the top of that hill over there and hide a while till the funeral's over. After they all go, fill 'er in."

Cladan headed up the hill of God's bony acres with Barry, the head gravedigger.

The open grave was eight feet deep. On the sides, rusty sheets of corrugated iron and old wooden beams held the hole intact by jacks so that it wouldn't cave in.

"Have a smoke somewhere," Barry wheezed at him, and wandered off.

There was a large rotunda, rows back, and Cladan was soon sitting inside it on his own, at the end of a long rounded bench seat by the open doorway, with a tall mud-caked spade at his side, looking out through a trellis, chain-smoking as he waited.

Pretty soon a slow procession of cars with lit headlights crawled through the gates and parked up front near the office, and the mourners in black slowly shuffled up the winding pathway, following the hearse snaking up the hill before them — a couple in the crowd, gratingly laughing.

Cladan leaned to one side in the rotunda, pulling his legs in out of view, lazily watching them all through a select diamond in the trellis, and slowly he began to drift as they dourly fumbled past him below like beaten dogs to the grave.

When the sermon began, Cladan was lying spread-eagled in the middle of the brick floor, staring up at the ceiling in a daze. There were no spiders or webs as he'd expected: just a conglomerate of thick rafters in the shape of the cross. He thought of all the old funerals he'd done as a boy, and he wondered about all the dead people of the world: an old priest he once knew when he was a kid who drank himself to death; the old lady on the bus who was always caked-up with make-up and forever mourning for everyone and the world; his dead sister; his dead steps; the dead Christ; thousands of slaughtered Kooris; zillions of butchered Zulus and Jews; all the children raped and strangled on the news; the recent rampages around town.

He lay there on his back, still as stone, like all the dead thousands in surround, feeling no different than when around the living. And he thought about that more particularly for a while, that maybe everyone was already dead, that maybe everyone had already been killed inside and were just wandering around on show for a while, just waiting to be imbedded as well. Or maybe it was just him all along. Maybe he was dead, he wondered, and not everyone else. But there's barely any room left for anyone now anyway. This cemetery was almost full.

"12 to go," Neil had said. *"Then we shut up the gates for good. The inn is full."*

Then a woman in the crowd suddenly howled uncontrollably, and Cladan bolted up straight from his thoughts and returned back to the bench, and quietly sat back down again and sadly watched them all again through the trellis. He lit another smoke and tried to blow out a diamond-ring for a second, then suddenly stopped, worried someone might spot him behaving so seemingly casual around death.

The woman's howls went on and on, getting more and more out of control; and then it started to ring false to him, as if she was putting it on. At first, it seemed that maybe all she wanted was the pity and the sympathy. Then he thought maybe it was the first chance she'd ever had to get a little attention since her spouse had passed on. Maybe he'd never given her a chance to get a word in edgewise with anyone, and she was relieved that he was finally out of her hair. Or maybe she'd treated him like a dog and never gave him a chance to open up, and was simply trying to atone for that. Or, secretly, she knew she'd get a lot of money now, so she was putting on a whole production to look less the gold-digger at heart. Or maybe she really did miss him already. Or maybe she was just an old aunt or emotional cousin who suddenly recalled that old joke he always used which never failed to get a laugh.

Who exactly this woman was he knew he'd never work out, but she seemed far too upset for anyone to comfort her.

Then he looked away, biting at the skin around his nails. Grief scared him, like it always did, soon as he ever got the slightest whiff of it.

Then they all sang a touching song he'd never heard before, though he didn't understand the language.

Looking at them all from such a distance he couldn't work out what country they were all from. They were all Indian, or Sri Lankan, or maybe even Jamaican, Cladan initially thought. And he looked down at the bricks in the floor, listening to the mourners tones wavering in such beautiful harmony, and he smoked again, and soon realized they were a Pacific people, and the sad island song ringing out soon set him to dreaming, as old memories of death and his mangled family seemed to jell in all the loose cracks of mortar weakly holding everything together at his toes. He'd only just recently visited his ailing ma, when oddly the phone rang when he was there, and he picked it up for her. (It rarely rang.)

"Hello?"

There was a long drawn-out silence, then a man said: *"Is that... Cladan... by chance?"*

"Speaking," Cladan said, surprised.

"This is the other Cladan."

Cladan was struck dumb for a moment, realizing his father was on the line. He hadn't heard his odd voice in near a decade. But, he reacted coldly in the end, and robotically said *"Don't' ever call again,"* and quietly placed the phone down. *"Telemarketer,"* he said to his ma.

After the mourners had left the grounds Barry appeared from behind a tombstone, stretching and yawning and rubbing his eyes, and he whistled Cladan over from the rotunda.

Lying at the bottom of the grave was a shiny brown coffin with a giant wreath of colourful rhododendrons on top, and assorted tossed singular daffodils.

But Barry soon left as a younger digger arrived to help instead.

Andrew turned his radio on, and he and Cladan began to slowly fill in the hole.

The first heavy yellow clumps of clay hit the wooden casket like a bass drum, and those first initial beats of falling earth seemed to long peal in Cladan's ears after this taxing week of work was over and his rent was paid.

As he watched for the last knitted flower of the wreath to be covered, Andrew told him all about mourners as they shoveled the earth back inside itself.

"There's a place where you can hire them for the day."

"Wha?"

"You can get the works. Six old women tag along and howl 'emselves wild."

Cladan was taken aback by this, but pretended not to be.

"To open up the others?" he mumbled back.

"Yeah," Andrew snorted, with a smile. *"They're called placebos. But they're more laxatives really, to help them move on."*

Cladan grinned. *"Some dress in black all their lives and mourn, don't they?"*

"Crazy," said Andrew, shaking his head. *"See, death don't mean nuthin'. You're gone."*

Cladan remained quiet for a long while as they both slowly shoveled in the clay, thinking about the whole mystery of death and what people believed in or didn't.

"Once, at school, we studied Gulliver's Travels, I think it was," Cladan said, vaguely thinking back to his favorite days at school.

"The giant, oh yeah."

"The teacher told us the author was Dean of St. Pat's in Ireland as well."

"Was a priest as well?"

Cladan nodded.

"But she said something about what he said... about death."

"Whasat?"

"I think it went, 'If providence designed something such as death... it cannot possibly be an evil to mankind."

Andrew didn't reply, and only raised an eyebrow in thought, nodding his head, and resumed work, wiping sweat off his face.

"Something like that," Cladan said.

Soon, Andrew started whistling along with an old melancholy song on his tinny radio. And he turned it up loud as the hot summer sun roasted them raw and they filled in the last hole of the week.

"I got you / That's all I want."

The greatest evil that can befall a man
is that he should come to think ill of himself.
Goethe

18

FINK DOGS AND PRINCESSES

As hail pelted down across Melbourne on the first night of summer a loose crowd of old warhorses in a distant bayside branch of the RSL sat primed at every table, ready to lap up the safe nostalgic air of a time long gone. Hot roasts were being served, and everyone was already sipping at their third beer in the mugginess.

Cladan rushed inside — half-drenched and slightly late — with the twisted frown worked up in his car set fully across his dial: his eyes unblinking, his nostrils flared like guns, and his mouth gripped tight as a wick in a candle vice. He'd just driven 50 k's in the storm in his clapped-out bomb for an interview to be a roadie for a band: it was nearly a year since his last job and he was desperate to get anything.

But he wasn't told it was an RSL, and only found out once he'd parked. His heart sank on seeing it: he thought it might've been an old beachfront pub with a young band starting out.

The instruments had already been set up on stage and he soon met Hap and the rest of the band in the wings — Stol and Moss the guitarists, and Cack the drummer. He'd spoken on the phone with Hap earlier in the day after spotting the job in the paper, and at Hap's suggestion driven all the way around Flip Bay to see them play and to get a taste for what the job might entail, considering he'd no experience.

"Found your way here okay?" Hap asked, shaking hands with him.

Cladan nodded, taken aback at how old Hap was.

"Sorry I'm late. There's a real storm out there. Big accident in Frankston."

"Frankston IS an accident," Hap joked.

"Yeah," Cladan smiled.

"Great start to summer, ay?" Hap said.

But Cladan's spirits had sunk further, on discovering everyone in the band was 30 years older than him, and they all had dyed hair and eyebrows, and he could instantly feel there was not only a distinct gulf between he and them — the way they saw the world, and regarded it — but between themselves as well. Everyone seemed surly with each other from the word go, as Hap showed him the amps and all the gear up on stage whilst sorting out the set list of songs they'd do for the show. Curious, Cladan glanced at their repertoire, only to find old John Denver relics, Pilot's "January", "Achy" stinking "Breaky", and a dozen other standards he'd always despised, like "The Pushbike Song" and "Me And You And A Dog Named Boo."

Fucking covers band, he thought — *RSL. What else? Bastard should've told me on the phone.*

As they all headed for the dressing-room door, Cladan quickly poured a squash from the jug on the band's table as offered, and went in with them to meet Hap's wife, Gilly, and their four screaming brats, who were sitting around a table stacked high with nappies; whilst squatted amongst them all like a revered Buddha was an obese white-haired woman in red, with a mole between her eyes like a third eye, and a missing front tooth, who was introduced as the children's nanny. Introductions were made, but soon enough family issues were being aired.

"'Fraid there's no seats left," Hap said to Cladan. *"Park yourself there, if you like,"* pointing out a small set of dead-end stairs away from everyone else. *"We won't be long."*

So Cladan shyly sat to one side on his own, feeling more aloof than ever, wondering if he'd just goofed badly in showing up, because his gut was telling him he just didn't belong there, and he knew he'd never be able to connect with them all as their own personal roadie. He made fleeting small talk with them all, trying to get along, but soon clammed up, feeling even more miserable than before he'd left home.

Then the band changed into their matching outfits. Cuffed orange shirts knotted in with K-Tel Technicolor ties, under luminescent gold vests covered in sequined butterflies and hummingbirds. And baggy raspberry pants with sparkling silver shoes. Bull-necked Stol, with jowls aflabber, had a long platted ponytail tucked down the crease of his spine, and a dangerous look in his eye. Clearly, he'd once led a wilder life, and it showed — but now he was probably doing the one thing in his youth he'd long despised before the realities of life had finally swamped him in, probably debt.

Moss was as skinny and emaciated as a junkie, with a greying near-Hitleresque moustache, and he had a horrible hollow laugh like he was dead empty inside — his mooing tone echoing everywhere like a heifer on a hill. And poor old Cack, the fat, moustached drummer with all his ringlets and bangs, couldn't stop preening at his beer-bottle body in the full-length mirror as he dressed. Cladan thought he looked like a walrus decked out as a gigolo.

Tanned good-looker Hap wore an iridescent blue shirt to stand out as the front man. It had little chrome edges on the tips of the collar. He looked like some star straight out of a soap opera: the blow-waved hair, the glow-white smile, the whole blinged-up bit basted down in concrete. He was the bass player, as well as chief crooner and top dog. His adoring wife Gilly was probably a model in earlier times, but she had a mouth that could never quit. She was the sort of grouch that chews everything quick and always spits out things way too fast, before checking anything at the door, so that no one gets trashed in the runoff.

But everyone loosely chatted, cracking tired jokes amongst themselves. Though the atmosphere was strangely dour.

Cladan couldn't imagine such a lack of spirit in a dressing room before a show. It was like sitting in a waiting room at the dentist's. There was an obvious reticence there; a distinct reluctance. It was clearly just a job to them all. There was no thrill in it for anyone anymore. Vacuum in a show biz B life, retrograde.

Then it was show time, and everyone filed out like they were being led to the gallows.

God of death, Cladan thought — sniffing at the mothball spoors in the air — *nail this box down on the lot of us, Thy Will Be Done.*

He could almost hear the crickets rubbing up their tiny knees as they stepped out to the audience. The place was dead. The band weren't even acknowledged, let alone noticed as they got up onstage. Cladan sat to the side at the band's table in the shadows, with Gilly, the nanny, and the kids. But when the band started up, it just made him gag. Grinning dish boy Hap pranced around on stage in such a smarmy way it was embarrassing — whilst from the sidelines, his wife beamed up at him loyally. Cladan had the feeling she'd fallen in love with Hap 10 years earlier as a fan, and was still that way, like the world hadn't budged an inch since.

The music was sheer torture to him. Old country standards he'd loathed since he was a kid. "From A Jack To A" fucking "King". Maudlin Humperstink odes. Sad old Moss moaning out "Honey Don't". And then when they played the lamest version of "Venus" he'd ever heard, he thought the lot of them should've been shot on sight. He felt blatantly offended, but just stayed put there, sitting at one end of the table, away from all the others, with his elbows on his knees as he watched the band. He was trying to work out just how the hell he could ever stomach working for them all, sitting through hours and hours of these grueling sets each night, listening endlessly to the same old songs he'd always loathed. He seemed to be in shock, and wasn't talking to Gilly or the nanny anymore as he juggled it all around in his head. And soon the kids had pulled back and were just staring on at him like he was a freak.

He felt like he hated them all, and that they all hated him back, and for a while there he joined in beating up on himself as well, just for something to do, whilst in the background "Ob-La-Di, Ob-La-Da" went on and on ...

Later on, for some reason not immediately clear to him, there was a sudden rush to finish the set on time. Everyone at the table, and at all the other tables beyond the dance floor, including all the waiters and bartenders bunched up at the bar, had their eyes glued to their watches like it was Ground Zero. Gilly and the nanny were virtually timing the band, and the band sped up a song and sloppily cut to the end quick in the middle of a verse, then rushed offstage and disappeared on the dot of nine as all the lights flipped off, and an old voice from above commanded, *"Everybody rise!"*

All the drinks were downed in one collective scull as everyone got to their feet in seconds, and turned to face the back wall of the hall where a crucifix glowed in the silence above the heads of everyone. Cladan followed suit, out of reflex, like it was an old order barked from the pulpit in church when he was a kid. Then the voice intoned a prayer about all those fallen in war, and everyone was murmuring back something, but Cladan couldn't make it out. He suddenly felt like he was an altar boy again, and it started messing about with his head. But the cross soon faded, and the voice lamented the setting of the sun over the battlefields. And it glowed again, defiantly, when it mentioned the coming of the dawn, and the rapture of all those wearied souls brought back to the bosom of the Almighty — and everyone slurred back their *"Amens"*. Then it snuffed out, and as the lights came up again, everyone turned, and sat back down to their meals and tucked in again, drinking and talking and laughing, as the band stepped back on stage and played The Shadow's "Foot Tapper" like nothing had even happened.

The whole interruption took about one scotched minute of eternity, and everyone was happy again like they'd just cleansed themselves and were suddenly redeemed of all sin and ache in the world. All of which suddenly instigated in Cladan the uncommon power of speech. He leant in over the table and spoke loudly to the nanny over the music.

"What was all that about?"

"It happens at every RSL at nine on Sat 'day nights."

"Why nine?"

"The sunset."

"Oh," he said. *"Whyzat?"*

"The dead," she said, as if it was the most stupid thing she'd ever heard.

Though that didn't clear anything up for him, he took it all as a welcome break from the monotony — at least it stopped the band for a while, let alone the relentless plastic gnashings of a hundred dentures in a grinding fest from wall to wall. And the nanny looked happy. And everyone else looked happy, with all their smiling faces everywhere. Then they all sat back like zombies again and watched the next set.

"Eye Of The Tiger"

"S-S-Single Bed"

Bobby Goldsboro's "Honey"

Soon, it was making Cladan's guts churn, just watching them play one despised piece after another. At one point, all three guitarists moved in close together, swinging back and forth in synch as they played, like a bunch of hyped-up teens with air-guitars in their bedroom after school: Status Quo for the fucking status quo. He couldn't believe it. He wanted to get a drink at the bar, but didn't want to appear a boozer in front of them all because he really needed the job. He was trying to appear the way he really wasn't, because he thought it'd be the only way he'd ever get a foot in the door, but the band was killing him. They all looked so old and ridiculous as they did all this stage business done to death a million years ago.

For a while he sidetracked himself by watching the crowds on the dance floor. They were soon stepping out in pairs, with hands cupping waists, and waltzing pleasantly about, letting loose great wafts of mothball fumes into the air, tinged with lashings of Old Spice and Californian Poppy — all the ancient R & R scents of the wars. A middle-aged couple whizzed around like it was an old bebop contest, but overall it was the grey-haired set not knowing how to move their legs anymore; all wooden steps, with eyes glazed, and fragile smiles. Though they were all really happy and enjoying themselves, Cladan found something terrifying about it all. Like it was a death march. The Reaper whistling while they sowed.

He chewed over the name of the band for a while: Hap Booker and the Hurley-Burleys. What was that? It gave no real clue they only did covers. If he'd known that, he wouldn't have driven 50 k's on the last of his petrol, just to be let down from the start.

Melancholy, bored, and excruciatingly sober, he soon started dreaming up new names for the band to pass the time...

A Thing Seen
Whole Hearts Climb
Miss Red Bilge And Her Bitter Zeal
The Mippy Dip Kerflanga Worry
Neck And Neck
Smell The Angels
The Gymps Of Tarax
City Speak
One Minute To One
A Pesky New Pollutant
The Morgue Belt And The Pressure Pattern
In My Water
The Great Fuck Out
Unction Of A Ghost
Sunday Still
The Moss-Farming Mummy-Unravellers
Black Market Reps
The Wrong Dog Is Buried
A Thousand Thousand Things
Symbol And A Half
Sin Seer
The Guerilla Den
Under A Hundred Summers
Block And Tackle
Snookah
Hair Of The Dog
Skulking Vulvi!
The Dead Thumbs Of The Damned

Plamma
Trenchmouth And Fuckface
Deja View
Adenoid And The Suck Merchants
Black Champagne
Rhizomes
The Diseasing Could
Fugitive Instance
Barking Lessons
Cheap Terror
The Great Unwatched
Ipsofucto
Fingers And Teeth
Spinning Jenny
Burgomaster
The Butcher's Loon
Kuntract
Swank In Hell
Mary Had A Leg Of Lamb
White Bat
Sic (sic)
Fistula
Tricked Fetuses

Remnants of surviving families were scattered around tables celebrating milestones with their remaining loved ones. A few half-baked emissaries came up to the stage and requested the band to sing "Happy Birthday" to Millie's umpteenth year on earth, who sat shyly in a corner sipping on a deep sherry.

And then there was a call from the other side of the floor — it was Raeline's 68th.

Both girls were duly obliged as Hap croaked out "Happy Birthday" to both of them.

Separately. One at a time. The song in full.

Twice.

Hell just went on forever.

Cladan couldn't believe the passion for that pissant tune, considering the age of most of them. Someone should've taken a stand, he thought, and shouted, *"Shut that fucker up!"* At least one of them. They were all old enough to know better.

Millie got a cake with a thousand flaming torches wheeled to her table, and Hap count-downed her to the blow out, and as she puffed up, Cack did a deep roll on his toms, and then when wheezing Millie let it all go, the flames disappeared in a flash with a crash of cymbals, followed by a round of staged applause from the management at the bar — all of them slyly guzzling themselves numb in the shadows.

Then Cack hit the skins and started singing "Mustang Sally", and Hap invited the two drunken birthday girls up on stage to whine the chorus with him, and they gyrated out of time, swiveling their hips about, wailing out of tune. But no one moved an inch from the tables, and the dance floor remained barren.

Cladan was still sitting miserable in the exact same spot as before like he was paralyzed, stubbornly unchanged, disgusted with himself, and even more repulsed by everything else around him — and knowing just outside the door was the world, felt not much better for it.

"Do you drink beer?" Gilly barked at him from the other end of the table.

"Like a fish," he blurted back.

"At least you've got something going for you," she said with a sneer, and looked back to the band.

Lovely, Cladan thought — *yet another endearing impression I've made on someone.*

So, as usual, he clammed up for good after that and just sat there and burrowed back deeper into himself.

Gilly just looked up in adoration at her husband on stage, watching him grinding hips with Stol, who seemed long beyond matters of conscience anymore. "Integrity" was probably the only really dirty word to him now.

Then, to top it all off, as Moss began to play a lead break, Hap knelt down in front of

him and pretended to eat at his strings — ala
Bowie on Ronson — as they played "Tie A
Yellow Ribbon Round The Old Oak Tree".

F-u-c-k-i-n-g J-e-z-u-z, Cladan implored to
above — *kill me stupid right now and bury me
without a fucking stone.*

At the next break he went and fetched that
beer and watched them all from the bar for a
moment. Gilly was videoing her kids playing
on the dance floor, though when a strobe light
started spinning colours across the waxed
floorboards she turned away, pinching at her
nose, as if it dizzied her.

When the band took their seats, Cladan
returned to the table and sipped at his beer
amongst them all again. Though why, he
wondered minutes later, he ever went back
there when he was so close to the front door
escaped him. He felt like he was trapped or
bewitched or cursed or something. The band
just sat around the table like beaten dogs,
mumbling nothing of consequence to each other.
They'd heard it all before. Sometimes everyone
just sat there in total silence, saying nothing,
and stared back across the dance floor at all the
pensioners spilling peas onto the floor.

Moss was on his second glass of cheap port from the bar. Cack was catching a nap in the shadows. And Stol disappeared out the back like he did every hour or so — probably to shoot up. Cladan had told the barmaid he was with the band, to get that beer on the house, but was told only lemon squash was free. Or *"Yellow coke"* as the kids called it.

Hap suddenly sidled up to him.

"I'm investing in a new state-of-the-art computerized lighting system soon, where I can program our songs to set lighting patterns. But it's expensive, so I've got to settle with doing it manually for the time being."

He had a series of buttons at his feet when he sang, and when he'd begin a certain ballad, he'd flick a switch with his toes and the lights on both sides would flick off the band and a yellow light would focus just on him alone as he crooned to everyone oblivious of him. All the equipment was Hap's. The instruments. The lights. The P.A. He had a station-wagon parked out back with a long boxed stainless steel trailer hooked to the back of it to store it all — like the sort quarter-milers use to cover their dragsters in transit. He'd got it all worked out. This was his living. Forget art, or even the notion of catharsis.

He didn't have a single axe to grind about the world and what it does to you.

(((DIZ PAYZ DA BILLZ AND FILLZ
ALL DA BABEEZ BELLEEZ)))

But Cladan soon felt guilty about thinking so ill of them all.

"Wish I could do something," he said to Hap, *"instead of just sitting here the whole night, watching on, doing nothing."*

"That won't last long," Hap said loudly above the brief blast of muzak and pokies in the background as a door was opened and closed. *"In a few weeks I'm getting a nifty top-of-the-range spotlight and I'll have you spotlighting my face all around the dance floor as I go from table to table doing my floor show."*

And that's when Cladan sort of first felt his blood drain. It may have been an arm, or a leg at first, he wasn't sure, but some trapdoor inside him just dropped open, and he suddenly felt giddy and more than a little faint, like the last dregs of his life force was being sucked from him and syphoned off back into the ether.

For a second, he reasoned it could well have been the lone beer that triggered it, on top of his empty stomach, and his nerves — he couldn't pinpoint it — but one thing he could zero in on was that the notion of ever having to follow Hap's vain *General Hospital* face around with a spotlight all night long as he crooned all his white-bread tunes was an impossibility.

He realised then and there, in concrete terms, to ease his conscience, that much as he desperately made the effort to get a job, there would be no chance in hell he could ever roadie this band. There was no way he could ever sit and listen and watch hours of the same old sad grind every night, with all those rotten songs, streaming out of that cheesy, holy roller hole, as he browbeat a crowd, vaingloriously embalmed in a time warp, built on the bartered corpses of their youth to save an Empire!

"Do you do any of your own songs?" he asked Hap.

Hap sheepishly ummed and ahhed.

"You have to do what people know. We're here to entertain them. Make them feel good. Not please ourselves. That's suicide."

And though he sounded sort of naively noble in a strangely chivalrous, old-fashioned way, Cladan couldn't help but think what Hap was engaged in in the long run was in fact the very sacrifice he most feared indulging ...

It was the penultimate set and the band inevitably played the dreaded "Achy". It was all suddenly clear to Cladan: God was in hell and the whole world had been sold off like a rotten pudding. Half a dozen wrecks were line dancing, including Gilly, the nanny, and the kids. People watched on transfixed like they'd just witnessed the birth of the aeroplane. A fat middle-aged man taught an old couple the moves.

"They're the same steps all the time, just in different directions."

Everyone watched all those good at it, trying to join in, but turned out of synch everywhere, tangling up all the other couples.

Cladan wished he was drunk. He could see nothing but death all around him; the dance floor a Spirograph of varicose veins, with the gentle clumping of orthopedic shoes being dragged through stray trails of dribble.

He was still sitting alone at the table in his invisible cocoon, with an empty glass, rolling yet another smoke, thinking of how to get out of there. He couldn't stand it anymore. He felt like he was going crazy. And then the band played a censored bubblegum version of "Walk On The Wild Side", and that's what really sealed the deal for him in the end. He realised these people were just plain fucking vampires.

He thought of just walking straight out the door, with no explanation: they didn't deserve one after butchering that song. But he caved in to too much mulling time, as usual, and suddenly the set was over and the band were slumping back down at the table again, saying nothing to each other — just like he'd done all night long himself. He knew they were all just as dead as he was inside. It was like the whole place was dead. Like the whole world was dead. The lights would only have to blink off again and all you'd hear are the worms outside baying for the old meat to finally come out.

During the earlier strains of *Achy*, Cladan had rammed his tobacco into his jacket so he wouldn't look like he was packing up when he chose to go. He just couldn't pluck up the nerve to cross the dance floor and walk out on them all like that. At least they'd given him a shot. He went over to Hap and Stol, who were fiddling with the PA, and just said, *"I've got to go. I've got a headache. Thanks a lot anyway. And all the best for the band."*

Stol looked like he understood completely. Cladan didn't say goodbye to Gilly or the nanny or the kids, or to Moss or Cack in back of him. He gave them all a quick wave and scrambled out of there as fast as he could and drove home in the hail, along the long rounded shore of Flip Bay, hounding himself for not fitting in with anyone again, cursing at Gilly's attack, praying for the car to survive the long trip back.

"What are you doing?" he screamed at himself in the racket, trying to get the heater going, tearing strips off himself all the way home as his empty stomach rumbled on.

"You stupid... job snob... song snob... fucking miserable turd! You're broke!... I should just slam this thing into a fucking tree!"

19
SLIPSHOD INVASIONS

Inside the circle nothing happened. Everyone just looked. A policewoman smelled the air then everyone did. As the crowds grew deeper, drivers slowed to a crawl, downing windows to stare. Then crime tape was strung across the road and everyone was moved away. Most went back to their cars and drove off. Some continued their strolls. A few local winos hovered nearby. But Cladan went too. He didn't know what had happened but it seemed a worry to all the other locals still out chatting on their porches. Maybe it was a gas leak, because the police were sniffing. A few were talking of another murder/suicide pact just like in the back street the week before.

Cladan headed back to his flat with the beer and watched the box for an update, surfing channels, but there was no mention of it. He could hear a few locals still on about it outside next door. Then the phone rang in the kitchen.

"Is Gorm there?" a woman snapped, in a husky voice.

Cladan wanted to pretend to be Gorm for a joke, but she sounded cold.

"Wrong number," he flatly said.

Downing his last beer, he went off to bed.

Never a day more trite, he seethed to himself, fed up — hoping to sleep properly for once. And he weakly dozed off with the hall light on through a crack in the door.

It was a crisp night, and he was wearing his pajamas, which were warm but too big. He'd often get the old fear at night, thinking the bed was full of bugs just waiting to scuttle up his legs to eat through his arse, and chew their way up to his mind — much like the 101 torture trick but without the cage and the rats. Sometimes it'd go on all night. Other times, his pillows were at fault, with the corners poked up like pert breasts against the moonlight streaming in through the blind, which was never much help when lonesome at night.

A few hours later he slipped back into his clothes and took off in his car to get more tobacco. He soon ended up sitting at a local beach, guzzling on a bottle of port from the boot of the car, and just listened to the waves lapping on shore, staring up at all the stars.

Then a little way away a drunken gang raced across the sand and threw someone in the shallows, and Cladan moved back to the stone wall in the shadows and watched them all skylarking about as he swigged. He thought about a group of friends he'd just suddenly walked away from, and how he knew that another group would never fill that vacuum of closeness again; and he knew that loss would probably colour every moment of his life to the end. He knew it wasn't just an odd patch, or a phase he was going through, to just cut himself adrift like that; it was an intentional act, a self-inflicted wound, and a visceral scarring he knew would be with him in every step to the end. It was an assault, dismemberment, self-sabotage, a veiled attack on himself, to hold back anyone from ever getting near him again.

They're all cheats anyway, he thought to himself — stumping at each other's squeeze when given the chance. One dud amongst them all scuppered who he thought he might wind up wedding — so he dropped the lot of them all in one gulp. It was all just poisoned after that.

What's the point of getting close to anyone again? They're under your skin in no time like a louse anyway.

It wasn't the racket of the traffic, or the trams squealing by his door, but the old phone ringing out in the kitchen that roused Cladan from his bed. He was surprised it was light out, and turned to check the alarm, to learn that not only had his head turned to lead, but morning had just flipped to afternoon.

He staggered with eyes closed down the hallway, bouncing wall to wall, with his toes all tucked in and curled, and he picked up the phone, pretending to be Gorm from the night before, strangely hoping it might be that woman again, his head grinding like stones.

"Gorm's dorm."

"Where in almighty fuck are you?" seethed his boss, the sack merchant.

"Wha?"

"I'm ringing all morning!"

"Why?"

"Get in here!"

"It's Saturday."

"It's fucken Friday!"

Cladan held his sore head, suddenly unsure.

"Is it?" he weakly said.

"All fucken day!"

"Ohhh..."

"Jee-zuz sucking bananas! After every pay night!"

Fed up, Cladan slowly closed his eyes, then dropped the phone back on the cradle and yawned all the way back down the hallway, punctuating it with an unraveling scream at the end, cursing his boss and every other small-time twerp he'd ever drudged for.

"Burnt dust on a busted brain!"

He soon got all warm back under the doona in the sunlight again, and almost fell back to sleep; then suddenly he burst out laughing at the top of his lungs, but soon stopped just as quick again.

Did I laugh out loud? he wondered, *or in my head?*

Then he realised he'd just blown another job, and it was the worst thing he could've done: he barely had a cent after the rent, and there wasn't a scrap of food in the place.

But he didn't care anymore.

Fuck 'em all. I'm going to die happy here alone, he thought to himself — *like old Gammy in a single bed.*

So he stayed tucked in bed with his hangover for the rest of the afternoon, listening to the phone still ringing out in the distance, pretending he was Gorm taking every call, laughing his head off, knowing it was never for Gorm, but for him.

Later on, there was a sudden knock at the front door, which interfered with everything. Cladan waited for more, and more soon followed, but louder, and more insistent. He just froze in bed, wondering who it could be. His boss could never get away from work, so it wasn't him. Fed up with more guesswork, he suddenly sprang down the hallway in quick successive strides like a cat — as his toes were now well and truly spread — and he quietly approached the door, gently peeking through the peephole.

A towering woman was standing in the corridor, with a black beehive hairdo, powdered white face, and black lips and eyelids everywhere. It shocked him at first, and he spied on her giant fisheyed face again because she was so striking. Even when she knocked again, he kept on looking at her, feeling the vibrations of the door against his lashes. But after a moment, he tucked in his pajamas and opened the door wide to her.

She looked at him, and what he was wearing, just as inquisitively as he looked at her and the green velvet gown she had on. But she was much taller than Cladan, and he was barefoot, and because he'd hardly stood up for the entire day, he felt much smaller than he usually did.

"Gorm?" she asked, her voice breaking in a hoarse tone.

Cladan recalled her husky voice on the phone the night before, and for the hell of it picked one of the cheesiest characterisations of Gorm he'd invented in bed to break the ice.

"Tis I, Mr. Less," he rasped, holding back a laugh just straining to explode. *"Unless you're a friend,"* he said, shyly smiling, near blushing.

With a shy smile back, she handed him a note, which fell to the floor between them, and Cladan politely bent over to pick it up, noticing it was blank on both sides as it fluttered about as it landed, but he reached for it anyway.

Then she pulled a screwdriver out of her bag and struck it down into the round of his back, sinking it in to the hilt. And he slammed down face-first to the floor with a scream as she scrambled inside the flat, her black soldier boots missing his face by a hair . . .

The day outside quickly shifted like it did every hour or so in Melbourne. The sunshine had gone for the umpteenth time and the clouds had rolled back in like a tide, sprinkling the gentlest of rain. The flat had darkened, and the front door was closed, and Cladan was sprawled on the floor in a pool of blood. But he soon stirred awake on hearing the phone ringing out in the kitchen — pains exploding across his body like bombs. He clawed himself along the hallway, smearing blood in his wake. He could see that the flat had been ransacked and trashed. He struggled to his knees by the stove and grabbed at the phone: it was his boss again, inflamed.

"So you've quit, hey? You're gunna do more than quit! I'm gunna rip the veins out of your body and skip down the fucken street with them! I'm gunna chop off your arms and legs and build a chair! Do you hear me, you pig-lazy slob?!"

"I'm bleeding," Cladan choked into the mouthpiece.

" You expect me to swallow that for being ...six hours late?"

"It's everywhere!" Cladan yelled, looking back at his blood smeared all over the lino behind him.

"From what, fucken shavin'?"

But a shooting pain in his side suddenly dropped him to the floor, and the phone dangled over the bench, knocking between the legs of a stool like a grandfather clock.

"I've had it with your pox excuses!" his boss bellowed down the line. *'I feel sick today. I vomited all night. I have diarrhoea. My daddy's dead!' I've heard 'em all!"*

But Cladan didn't answer.

"You there? Cladan?" he roared. *"If you're shitting me, and I call out an ambo, I'm out a thousand right there! You know that! I'm telling you, cheese me like this and I'll fuck you up! I mean it! Are you there? This is a big ask, you slack cunt of a throwback! Do you know how many briquette trucks are in today? I'm up to my fucken eyes in bags!"*

But there was nothing but silence.

"Cladan? Answer, you bastard! Right, fuck it. I knew you were goosed from the start. (CLICK) *Hang up now...* (CLICK) *I can't dial an ambo if you don't hang up!...* (CLICK) *You know the front phone's fucked!...* (CLICK) *I'm not going out the back!...* (CLICK) *Hang up, will you!...* (CLICK) *What, you're fucken crippled now?...* (CLICK) *Just hang the fucken thing up! I'm up to my eyes in bags!..."*

20
THAT FRIEND, GALORE

Cladan finally left hospital a few months after his assault, and was convalescing in his new flat on Anzac Day, but he still hadn't really got his head around all that had happened to him. He just sat there in his new digs, staring at the first beer he'd poured since the attack, admiring how the barley glistened like gold in the glass, and he placed it up on the sill by the pane, which was nothing but a giant blue sky. He thought it was the right time to celebrate and have a drink, and he took a giant gulp as he thought of his attacker again, and how they'd just got her the week before — or him, as it turned out. Kerold *"Go-Go"* Kerang: a local transsexual junkie on the double-cross with the wrong address.

In Cladan's stitched-up guts was now the donated kidney of a 33-year-old community stalwart from Warneet, who was run over by a glazier, and *"who,"* in the flippant words of his cheery surgeon, *"was not only a barista, but a barrister."*

Cladan had been comatose for months, and missed his own birthday, so he lifted his glass to the clear blue sky and toasted good riddance to his teenage years forever.

"Happy birthday," he said patronizingly to himself, as if it just had to be said aloud by someone, and he took another freezing gulp, wondering — *Or is this one forfeited if you're out for the count but you come back again?*

Down in the courtyard of the old block of flats all the neighbours were getting out and about on such a sunny national holiday, with all their cars zooming in and taking off. From the tall hickory trees flanking one side, a flock of shrieking white cockatoos left their perches and swooped down into the car park, then lifted up higher and soared across the sky, and when their echoing screams faded like the cries of pterodactyls, all the cicadas in the park in back resumed their song from an hour before.

Cladan gulped at his beer as he watched a long line of loud Harleys lean in to take the bend, and what looked like a dozen sloops racing across Flip Bay in the distance. Some of his neighbours succumbed to old sounds to soothe themselves on their day off. Dylan bled his harmonica out of one window, whilst Guy Lombardo chugged out of another. Over in one of the two corner flats without windows, The Stones were throbbing against the walls, making all the insects dance. But the sun beamed on, and the light beer flowed, and all the music jumbled together in the courtyard like the din of a dozen crashing worlds. And no one minded the racket for once. The saltbushes, long burnt by the sea winds, were glowing white near the half-melted bins. And all the dirty junk mail flapped about in their holes like smuggled birds. Everything was just birch dry and breezy. A lawnmower going off in the next street only made it all feel even more homey and cosy.

Cladan sighed out loud pleasantly. No more kneading flesh for saps. No more dusting turds for frauds. No more carrying slops to Gods. And no more bagging up the world.

He never felt so calmed. He felt like he had permission to relax at last, till everything was healed anyway. And the only thing to do was fetch another piss-weak beer from the fridge. But it seemed easier to smile, than frown, like it was before. After all that had happened, he felt like he might well be able to survive anything thrown at him now. The worst was done. It all had to be easier from now on. Then a blowfly whizzed by his face and circled the room, before buzzing up close to its reflection in the pane, and Cladan decided not to bother wasting time shooing off anything he could never control in the end, not caring whether it planted diseases all over the place so that he'd just rot to garbage. His body numbed by the sun, his mind spinning loose from all the ale, he dared it to drop its bundle wherever it pleased.

Nothing seemed to matter anymore. It was just so serene there, with the calming sea just across the road, and the giant blue sky everywhere, that he soon surrendered to daydreams like he did for so long in intensive care . . .

21

ALL THE LEAKING BEINGS

"A *new theory has emerged,"* said a newsreader on TV, *"regarding last week's stranding of 88 pilot whales at Hell's Gates in Tasmania. Locals believe it has everything to do with the booming gentrification of the western coast, where luxury homes dot the cliffs with large bay windows overlooking the Southern Ocean. It has been suggested that the high-pitched squeals from cleaning all these windows is in fact mimicking the calls of whales, and perhaps drawing in passing pods as they migrate to the nursery waters of the Great Australian Bight. Locals wonder what all these high-pitched window squeals might in fact be communicating to whales. Some claim it may be some sort of invitation for food, to come this way and hunt."*

Cladan span cold noodles around his fork and stabbed the last angel on horseback, then looked back to the TV, intrigued — only to spot out of the corner of his eye an epizootic rat with cat burglar feet crippling by the stove and entering the kitchen cupboard where the hot water tank was hidden. He'd just spotted its tail from the couch as he wiped sweat away from his face and swigged on a beer, the newsreader rambling in his ear.

"After the break, looking at clouds can give your eyes cancer..."

Then a World Vision ad came on about deformed Romanian kids and, forgetting about the rat for a moment, he just sadly watched the TV. Being a hot night, all the neighbours' windows were wound wide open in the courtyard, and he could hear them all sobbing inside their flats from seeing it as well...

Last week, in an old city pub, Cladan was put on the spot to play doubles in a game of pool with some old workmates he'd bumped into from way back in his first job — Speed, Nat, and Ring. They got into a rally like the old days, but Cladan copped out early, feigning asthma, and caught a bus home, feeling even more miserable.

"It is to love, than to be loved," a woman said to her friend beside her in the bus, as

Mozart blared out through the tiny speakers at the end of every seat.

"It is to understand, than to be understood. It is to forgive, than to be forgiven. It is to be self-forgetting, to really find. It is in giving, that we really receive."

They were both geed up to see what was at the end of the rainbow hanging over the next suburb. Smiles soon fell Cladan's way, and curious, when they got off ten blocks away, he got out too and followed them to go see as well. The rainbow ended under the West Gate Bridge in Hyde Street, Spotswood, but there was no pot of gold there — and Mozart's Symphony In F wasn't Symphony In Fuck, as Cladan's fantasy soon petered out.

Jesus, he thought, subtly watching them rolling around on the banks of the Yarra in their dresses, flailing about in long sumptuous kisses, hands everywhere — *they're all over each other like measles.*

But when they saw him they ran off laughing like mischievous nymphs.

On the way home again, he sat alone by a window at the back of the bus, feeling dour and even more strangely redundant, as the peak-hour commuters kept on jabbering, *"Look at that strange rain."*

22
DONKEY IN A WATER WHEEL

Cladan had shifted premises again, retreating to a cheaper suburb because of the recession, but there wasn't a job to be found anywhere and he was more depressed than ever. It'd been four days since he'd last stepped outside his door, and his new neighbours in the horseshoe-shaped courtyard could never make him out. At dusk, loud music would try to burst out of the confines of his flat, but the front door and windows were always shut as usual, and only a faint light ever escaped around the blind above the door.

A strolling couple with a pram suddenly paused by the block of flats, looking up the driveway, gossiping about the madman's place like everyone else.

"See the flat on stilts? The lone one above the carport? Don't linger, don't stare. Sometimes it knows. It chases everyone up the street, I swear!"

Come dawn, the low green sky spilled its guts everywhere, flooding the whole street, and all the drones in suits promptly left the other flats, one by one, launching rafts, paddling their briefcases to work — their wives waving them all off as they listened to the madman farting in bed through the brick wall.

Then at noon they'd hear the spluttering of eggs again, and the old clinking of knife, fork, plate, and sink; the same thing day after day.

And when dusk arrived, and everyone was back home from work, a splinter of light would flicker on above the front door, and stay on all night, with the blinds skimped shut like the eyes of a ray. Then morning, it was lights off and all blinds opened up again — the same old reverse and back.

Music blared at the oddest hours, as did the TV; or sometimes a drunken argument he'd have with himself when he was picking at some ancient wound again. Or suddenly, there'd just be his loud cackling laughter ringing out in the middle of the night.

Everyone in the street stirring awake in their beds, with the hair on their necks rising like reeds — some of them clutching at shivs under their pillows, just in case. And watching it all through a chink in the blinds, as the pale moon bounced like a song across their roofs, Cladan applauded it all in the dark like he was welcoming home a hero.

23

GO UP THE MIDDLE SIDEWAYS, NOT DOWNHILL

"SALES ASSISTANT.
EARN UP TO $60,000 P.A.
NO EXPERIENCE NECESSARY.
TRAINING PROVIDED."

Racing through the gears, Cladan dreamt of freeing himself from the limbo that now seemed his life. The ad had a blind sense of hope about it, he thought, mulling it over as he drove on towards the high noon sun. Maybe it was the chance he needed to finally emerge from the mud and begin his life afresh. Maybe he'd meet a girl; make some new friends. But were they really all that open to anyone turning up for the job?

He pulled up and parked by a row of old trees along St. Kilda Boulevard, right in front of a tall, white tiled building shimmering in the sun like a space shuttle.

The invisible beam caught his toes, and the doors parted as he entered, revealing a rotund guard seated behind a marble counter down the other end of the lobby. The guard put his hat on and looked closely at Cladan in his rags as he approached to sign the ledger, showing his I.D., stating what floor he was going up to, who he'd come to see, date, time; then he pinned a visitor's card to his lapel, strapped a chute on his back, and sent him up.

Cladan stepped out onto the top floor, where a wide corridor in velvet with crystal doors stretched out for all eternity. The receptionist looked up at him and handed him a clipboard. On a coffee table, *Time* magazine with a Middle Eastern butcher and his crusty nostrils on the cover, dubbed Man of The Year.

LIST REASONS FOR LEAVING
PREVIOUS EMPLOYMENT:
1)   Don't know.
2)   Bored.
3)   Stabbed.
4)   Went mad.

Cladan handed it back to her, holding the magazine over his face, softly babbling like a maniac to break the ice. But when he lowered it with a smirk, he could see she was plainly ignoring him as she typed — or maybe she had earphones on under her long hair, he wasn't sure. He sat back down in a cold sweat, soaked with self-loathing for trying to be funny again. It never worked.

Everyone wandered by in zillion dollar suits and shoes, with Ned Kelly glasses, and sculpted hairdos everywhere. He looked down at his scuffed shoes, with the soles thin as paper, and his faded black jeans with blotches of ash over the knees and crotch, and his old crumpled-up jacket like the screwed-up scraps the receptionist continually tossed in her wicker bin. Then the Commander approached, sticking a hand out to greet him — dismissing him in an instant, on spotting the rags and ratty hair alone — but he led Cladan into his capsule anyway, where they both sat back in tipped-up chairs, facing the moon through an aperture in the ceiling.

Cladan laid his cards down without delay.

"I'd need a few suits to get rolling," he mumbled, nervously. *"That's my only immediate concern, to bring myself up to speed,"* briefly mentioning he'd been out of the loop for a little while, without elaborating.

The Commander snorted as he read Cladan's resume, laughing out loud that he'd gone mad, and admitted as much.

"I tell the truth," Cladan said, with a wobbly smile.

But the Commander gently admonished him for that, pressing the point that he shouldn't always give things away so easily.

"Can't help that," Cladan snapped back.

Then the Commander suddenly turned all Samaritan on him, and talked down to him like he was a leper on his last legs. Cladan was soon blathering on about all his hopes and dreams for the world, and the Commander told him of all the old false hopes he'd once had in his youth as well — like how he was once an actor in Sydney years ago, and could've been the greatest star there ever was.

He soon handed Cladan a flip-top card with his name embossed, telling him to get back to him if he ever came up with something that might make a lot of money. And almost subliminally, Cladan was shaking his hand, and heading down the lift, and bidding farewell to the old fat guard squatted at his altar like King Tut crapping in a giant copper wok...

"WILD NEW THEATRE RESTAURANT.
BRANCHES IN TEXAS, AND HANOI.
NOW OPENING IN MELBOURNE.
NEED FULL STAFF.
BRING PROPS IF NECESSARY."

A racket of glib Americans were scattered about the foyer, loudly *"woo"*-ing into cellular phones, rolling out endless trails of laundered zeros. In dread, Cladan took the form to scribble down the history of his drudgery.

1) PORTER at the Bolt-hole Hotel, Pine Gap Joint Facility, NT, Australia. (Underground base, level 10: CLASSIFIED). Provided the service for such luminary guests as ███████████ ███████████ and ████████████████████ and several world leaders (reportedly deceased, of course) before their maiden flight to retirement village in cluster HD 23514, of the Seven Sisters, Pleiades. (Salary: CLASSIFIED.)

2/ GRAIN COUNTER at the Hula Hourglass House. Sifted through dunes of common yellow beach sands. Sieved through tonnes of the black lagoon pebbles of tropical Bali in Indonesia. High Achievement Award and Guinness Book of Records Distinction for counting 240 trillion grains. (Salary: $1000 per bushel.)

A Sasquatchan of a Texan with a beard down to his waist greeted Cladan at his desk with his resume — one hand out like the Commander, with the same dead look in the face. Cladan pointed out to him they were jokes, stressing he hoped it might enlighten him to the fact that he was *"a zany guy, perfect for your organization."*

The American glanced at his resume again, as if to reassess it all.

"What's Pine Gap?" he asked, quizzically.

Cladan tried to describe what it was, as far as anyone knew, but the American only read on without answering. Then behind them, a girl in a black cape belted out *Cabaret*, accompanied by a tape of timpani and triangles. Everyone watched her till the end and politely applauded. But Cladan got a *"we'll get back to you,"* in a cold Texan twang, and was suddenly out by the Yarra again, watching the balls ricocheting by in limed blurs...

FOR THEE, FOR THOU, FOR NOW, SO LONG

Soft rain falling in the night. The air thickening into a hot stew. The hope of recovery long gone. All the other skiffs tucked away in the sheds along the shore in an uncommon show of solidarity, empathy, and compassion.

The spirit of the place. The saddened town. The strangely calm and ironic sea.

Old relatives and family friends burying hatchets for a day. Cobwebs cut aside by all the tension. Spidery faces wilting loose from all the grief. Every familiar voice, a dull mazurka tone. Rings spinning over whitened knuckles. Odd cushioned attacks. Each sigh a disguise. Irreclaimable dolls engineered by the common stun of loss.

Elli's abandoned pug, scuttling lap to lap, a bag of nerves. A relative's schnauzer cowering under a chair, behind someone's legs, all eyes, petrified, as outside Elli's last galah screams up at the moon like a hound with its throat cut.

Cladan's old trampoline under the crabapple trees — still still, and filthy with years of leaves and dust. Night falling like a dirty parachute, thieving another killing day.

Cladan hoped that, somehow, after all the years that had passed, Haxt and Sunnie would appear out of the blue, and they would all be finally reunited again. But he was told that Haxt was now living overseas with his aunt and uncle, and it wasn't till days later that he learned Sunnie had taken her life the year before.

God, this whole botched family, Cladan thought, sadly pondering over the whole mess for the millionth time since he was a kid.

He remembered his ma's violent jokes, her white fingers in the cold, her crooked smile, the deep drags of smoke she always toked, and her plain discomfort when in the company of braggarts.

Alone in her kitchen, away from everyone else, Cladan lifted the old Mayan apron off the stove and looked at the colourful glyphs his ma always tried to unravel, frustrated she never understood it all, and he put it around his shoulders like the cape of a super hero, just like he used to do as a kid, hearing the tone of her laughter still on the air as he stared out the open back door like he could still fly away.

Cladan swore to himself that at the chapel in the morning he would not join in singing *Amazing Grace*. He will not ever, by any means, call the dead wretches.

24b
THE DAY HAPPENS TWICE

The rain roared down for the first time in months, and the thunder rumbled on for what seemed forever, as lightning ceaselessly cracked across the inky clouds. The escort had only left his hotel room an hour or so before. Cladan had sculled down five beers before she'd arrived, and now was on the last of the dozen overall. But he couldn't sleep, and just stared out the window in the dark, watching the light show, thinking about what a disaster it all was in the end. He still felt riddled with grief and was heading back home in the morning.

Chasing time, he drunkenly thought — *to just waste our souls away.*

He reached over and grabbed the hotel's last complimentary Tim Tam. As he slumped back down in a chair, he imagined he'd just tucked his young imaginary son into bed, and he started telling him the same old night story he remembered his own imaginary pop had told him when he was a boy to try to make him fall asleep when he felt lonely and sad.

In a slurring whisper, he told his son how everyone on this side of the world was trying to go to sleep as well, because it was night, and how everyone on the other side of the world was just waking up, because it was day. And how they'd all soon be so tired after school, or work, that they couldn't wait for the world to turn from the sun again, and for night to fall again, so they could all go back to sleep again, to rest, like all those going to sleep on this side of the world.

"Then later on, it did turn to night for them, and they all went back to sleep on that side of the world. Then everyone on this side of the world woke up, because it was day again. And that's always the way it is. Both sides of the world take turns like this, forever.

"Well, who wants to sleep in the day and be awake at night? You wouldn't see anything if you were only awake at night!

"Imagine throwing a stick with your dog in a park at night. Your dog might never find it. And you might never find your dog! But if your dog had a little light on its collar, like on

your bike, that would be all right. You wouldn't lose your dog, but what about the stick? And what about you? Your dog might never find you. So you'd have to wear a light too, like your dog. And the stick would have to have a light too.

"But what if everyone was out playing with their dogs at night at the same time? Imagine all the lights! And all the lost sticks! And all the lost dogs! And everyone calling out for their dogs at the same time! And all the dogs barking back at everyone at the same time! And all the people finding the wrong dogs! And all the dogs finding the wrong people! Way too confusing!

"It'd be better to sleep at night, and wait for when the sun was out to play with your dog. Then you could throw the stick as far as you wanted to in the park, and your dog would find it, and your dog would find you! So that's why everyone sleeps at night; so everyone can play with their dogs during the day.

"It's true! Haven't you ever noticed that dogs sleep at night too, like all of us do?

"Do you ever hear dogs barking at night?

"Of course not. They're all asleep! Like everything is! Even the sun sleeps at night.

"It's true!

"Well, have you ever seen the sun out at night?

"Of course not. It's asleep! Like you should be! Remember, never bother looking for the sun at night, because it's asleep. It's a waste of valuable sleeping time. Never look for anything at night! That's what the day is for! So you can find everything where you left it the day before, and the day before that, and all the days gone before that! So many days have gone by, and there's even millions more to come! And everyone knows it! Even the dogs know it! And the birds know it! And the sun knows it! Even the moon knows that!

"The moon?

"I forgot to tell you about the moon!

"The moon's a funny old thing, son. It's the only thing that sleeps in the day, and it's the only thing that stays awake at night. See? Look at the window. See it there? W-i-d-e awake. I told you. But do you know why the moon's always awake at night?

"Guess.

"You'll never believe it.

"Because it's afraid of the dark! Which is crazy! It stays awake all night long, and then suddenly, when it's day, and the sun wakes up, and the dogs wake up, and everyone else wakes up with it, the moon just nods off to sleep. And it never sees daylight! Never. I mean, what a thing to miss! That's why the moon's mad. Because everyone knows daytime is fun! You can see the blue sky, and all the rainbows and green trees, and all the people's smiles. But at night, you can't see the blue sky, or all the rainbows and trees, or all the people's smiles. So everyone just goes to sleep instead.

"But sleeping can be fun, because you can dream! And you can see daylight in dreams! That's the only way you can see the blue sky at night, and all the rainbows and trees, and all the people's smiles. So you can have two days in one, and you'll live twice as long!

"Dreaming is a very special thing to do, and a very important thing to do to be happy. So go to sleep, son, and dream! Your head's like your own TV set, and you can watch whatever you want. And guess what? You won't believe this. You won't. You can watch whatever you want, and ... with no ads!

"Can you believe it? None! No ads about dishwashing liquids, or funeral homes, or mustard eyelashes for cats! Nothing!

"That's right. You can watch anything!

"So go to sleep, and dream, and enjoy it. 'Night son.

"All this talking's made me feel tired myself. Pop's going to go to sleep too, and dream as well. And in colour, like you!"

But all the lightning kept on flashing into the room, and it suddenly made Cladan feel dizzy. Soon the room was spinning like a drill. Staggering quickly in the dark towards the bathroom door to get to the sink, he opened the wardrobe by mistake and vomited all over the robes and towels. And then he turned around and vomited all over the mirror and the door, and he couldn't stop vomiting as he tried to find a way out of the room ...

PART TWO

25
PING-PONG DEL ALMA

PERU ➤ When the annual spring meteor showers shot across the bow of the equator, Cladan drunkenly weaved through Customs like a lamb, following a dozen sunburned tourists in Hawaiian leis like him the same. Then they all went to Zoo Peru, and Cladan rushed off to see the greening sloths first, nibbling on a box of crackers, though he was getting a cramp from his money belt. Using his last dollars from the crime compensation fund for his assault, he'd decided to finally get away for a taste of the world and blow out all the cobwebs while he still had the chance. It was only after catching a story on the news about the birth of a two-headed striped tapir — soon slaughtered out of superstition — that he decided to go see the Amazon before there was nothing left of it. He'd always had a thing about it: the anacondas, the piranhas, the howlers across the sky. It was either that or go see the sphinx, and he couldn't afford to do both.

When he'd first arrived, the misty chaos of Lima had just flowered into the Lord of The Miracles Fiesta, and a million-strong crowd slowly moved through the city streets, dressed in violet, lugging icons on their backs in the sunshine. Lavender balloons were floating about everywhere, and a long line of shooting galleries, Ferris-wheels, and merry-go-rounds with smiling purple llamas hugged the Pacific shore for as far as could be seen. Vendors were hawking everything from idols of Incan gods, and bowler hats of the Sierra, to reed models of Lake Titicaca skiffs, and long whittled blowpipes from the jungles of the Selva.

Cladan wandered past a sea of tables outside a cafe where all the old retirees from his party were lunching on guinea pig and bananas, laughing their heads off; whilst all about them, money-changers swapped soles for greenbacks amongst the pickpockets, as a drunk leaned against a wall and took a siesta with his brim down and wallet gone. Then when the sun bottomed out, the swift winds chilled through across the Pacific, and all the tourists headed for the clubs for the night.

In one ritzy ballroom overlooking the ocean, a crowd of pensioners danced cheek to cheek under spinning fans as the waiters drifted by in white suits like ghosts, topping up piscos and dregs.

Cladan downed another guinda as he watched the rest of his party waltz free across the dance floor like no one else existed in the world. But he soon went up to his suite and headed for the view to have a smoke and hopefully spot some of the meteors everyone was on about all the time. He'd grown tired of the lot he was stuck with anyway. He'd had his fingers crossed at the start that he'd wind up with someone to pair off with — but they were all married couples, three times his age. There wasn't a thing he could discuss with any one of them, and he was simply looked on like some bewildered kid from nowhere.

Stepping out onto the balcony, and stretching a yawn, Cladan took a long drag of his smoke as he stared out through a break between buildings to the Pacific Ocean glistening in the distance like the upturned silver belly of a whale. He was thinking about how he'd set out in the morning the other way to see the ruins first, before heading inland through the Andes and finally out to the river.

He loosened the money belt a notch and felt his breathing getting easier. He'd never had that much cash on him before, and didn't imagine he ever would again. He felt like he really was on holidays — like the whole crowd he was traveling with were — and he secretly harboured the idea that there might just be a chance he'd stumble onto some out of the way place he'd normally never step into, where maybe he'd suddenly feel like he fitted in and belonged, and maybe get a job there, and settle down and start his life again. He was prepared to never return home again. There was nothing there for him.

He looked up at the sky, thinking about what the most bizarre breakfast might be on a menu in Peru — poached toucan eggs on toast with hummingbird kebabs?

Melbourne was only a slight birdcall in his brain now. The stopover in Hawaii alone blew all that out. He felt like he was closer to the world. But just as he turned to go back inside and refill his drink, he heard a whistling through the air, then something clocked him from behind, pushing him back into the suite. He staggered about for a second, looking around at the floor, wondering if maybe a bird or a bat had crashed in, or even the sliver of a meteorite.

But it was only when he glanced at his reflection in a mirror above the hearth, and turned to walk away, that it first stung, and he caught sight of it in profile — a long thin dart poking out of the middle of his back.

The old hotel doctor put Cladan to bed and harrumphed as he injected a giant hypodermic into Cladan's rear with a grimace.

"Six months now," the doctor said, straining, as he slowly pushed down the plunger. *"We know it is someone in the apartment building across the way. The road is littered with darts every day from hitting the side of the hotel. Trajectories are being studied as we speak."*

Cladan pulled a face in silence.

"It is a twisted world, senor, as you no doubt know. Perhaps a crackpot of the Senderos."

He looked at Cladan for a response, but Cladan was too busy clenching his face from the pain.

"Revolutionaries, senor." the doctor whispered, as the plunger slowly passed the halfway mark. *"They do not relent."*

"Is this a tetanus shot or what?" Cladan squealed with a tremor. Then he hollered out loud, *"Gee-ZUZ!"*

"It is an amalgam of tropical serums," the doctor said. *"A little harmaline. A booster to thwart various setbacks from arising."*

"Like what?" Cladan blurted, with tears in his eyes.

"Well, yes. Tetanus. Also rabies. Just in case. We cannot be sure the tip was not dipped in some strange concoction of animal fluids. In the Highlands, mad dogs, vampire bats, skunks and poisonous frogs are ensnared for such purposes and sold across the black market as a cheap munition."

"Will I be ok for my trip down the river?" Cladan said quickly, in agony.

"I will look in on you later, senor," the doctor said. Then he weakly smiled. *"But I don't see why not."*

Cladan frowned as he pulled up his trousers, then flopped back down on the bed, suddenly drained. The doctor closed his bag and got to his feet.

"My god," Cladan said, slightly worried, looking back at him. *"You're forehead's as tall as a door. Or is it an eyelid? ... Don't blink!"*

"The side effects are robust, senor."

Cladan looked around the room: everything was twice as tall, and five times farther away.

"Don't be alarmed," the doctor implored.

Cladan looked back up to him, and slowly blinked an eyelid, then just as slowly blinked the other.

"This is good. It has taken hold of exactly what it should. Your blood is fine and supple, senor. You will be feverish with dreams, but try to sleep. In days to come you will feel renewed."

"How now, Mary?" Cladan whispered back, suddenly terrified.

The doctor chuckled once up to the ceiling, and subtly crossed himself as he looked back at Cladan. *"Forgive me, but my name is Romoldo, yet you call me the Blessed name of Our Lady, senor. A most amusing serum, you must agree."*

Cladan only stared on in terror as the doctor smiled back at him.

"Your mind loosens," the doctor added.

"I want to put a hat on a treetop!"

"You may experience various delusions, episodes of startling delirium, but you will be fine, senor. I will look in on you at dawn. Now you must sleep."

"Shut the balcony door!" Cladan yelled.

The doctor unconsciously held up a hand as if just remembering, looking towards the balcony. The drapes were blowing into the suite from the shifting night breeze, but he walked the long way there, around the perimeter of the room, ducking his head in as he slid shut the door. Then he swooped back his mussed up grey hair, grabbed his bag, and moved to leave.

Cladan stared at him with bugged-out eyes. *"Don't bite my egg on me!"* he screamed.

The doctor waved back, stifling a snigger in his nose as he left the room. But soon as the door shut behind him, an iguana roared across Cladan's eyes like a lion at the start of an old MGM movie, initiating a sudden hallucination as his teeth began to chatter from the cold...

Cladan saw himself in a soldier's uniform, walking along a shore on the Galapagos Islands. Huge tortoises were slowly inching across the sand in the distance like ladybirds crawling across someone's back. Then he heard his own voice telling himself about the history of what had just unfolded, like he was narrating a documentary.

Butchered tourists lay scattered everywhere. There'd been a war instigated by an uprising of nature. Lava lizards had initially turned on everyone and all the albatrosses were plucking out the eyes of everyone scattered across the dunes. Man had turned on man. And now Cladan was the only one left of them. All he had left to his name was a broken bayonet. And the volcanoes "that were every island," were eerily rumbling beneath his toes. Soon, he saw himself at a lagoon, sharing fish with the cormorants; swimming, washing and wading in the sea with all the herons. Over time crabs no longer nipped at his feet because of their acquaintance. He could see himself playing with all the iguanas in the shallows; sitting amongst them all on the rocky shoreline at dusk, their eyes diluting with the waves, like an old bunch of wise Labradors watching the sunset. But the sun seemed more than a clock or a fire to them all — it was a friend. Then it was dawn again and he could see himself waking up on an old lava bed, only to find next to his pillow of kelp, a woman asleep. Initially, he wasn't shocked that she lay there, nor surprised that she lay there asleep, so he left her to let her snooze in peace.

Later, he was swimming along the lagoon, when suddenly he noticed her beside him again, bobbing as she stroked, and she too was naked. At dusk they were hunting along the wide stretches of the shore, bagging crabs, then boiling them up over a beach fire and sucking the meat out of all their legs. And in the twilight shadows they made sandcastles into a city and sat inside and watched the tide slowly tear it all down around them. But just as the sun quickly sank, and the moon rose, and all the stars appeared, she suddenly walked away and vanished. Cladan didn't know her name and she didn't know his, as they never spoke. Then the following dawn Cladan saw himself walking along the shore again, like at the beginning — hunting for rays with his broken bayonet. Then the woman suddenly appeared from nowhere and gently grabbed his helmet from his hand and they both quietly walked along in ankle-deep water, spearing and collecting their meals.

On waking from his dream — the Amazon no longer on his mind — Cladan could hear the roar of the iguana still reverberating through his ears like a distant thunder, loosening the jelly in his bones, and in odd flashes the skull of Charles Darwin with a long white beard was suddenly welcoming him in flitting cameos as he blinked. At first, he didn't know who it was, and initially thought it was God, then Galileo, Marx, Santa, Brahms, Rasputin and Ned Kelly. But after a while, he noticed the tiny heads of beagles in its eye sockets, and realized who it must've been all along. He stepped up to the balcony window in the dark and peered out through a slit in the drapes at the building diagonally opposite, trying to shake off the remnants of the vision — though Darwin kept on trying to sell *"U. N. pituitaries"* to him with every blink like a nagging ad.

"Naturally, you have five from wet to choose."

For a moment, he thought of the good old days of his youth when he was scholarly and worshipped the Animal Kingdom, and how he was transfixed by those few odd sanctuaries of the world's most unique beasts: Madagascar, the Galapagos Islands, home. On closer consideration though, he realized — and finally admitted to himself — his chief interest in the Amazon had only ever really been the piranha at heart. The odd thought of just throwing himself at them always sort of appealed to him — for a 30 second stint, all problems could be solved. But the Galapagos Islands had always been sacred to him as a boy. He'd often dreamt of riding the tortoises there, in one long dawdle along the shore, lying back against back in the sun. Or standing on top as a one-footed traffic cop, slowly passing by, making his family laugh. But he realized he wasn't exactly sure where the islands were, and referred to his tattered world map again, suspecting they lay somewhere near Spain, only to learn they were the Canary Islands all along — which was a shock to him, as he'd always thought he was a wiz at geography. Then he was tracing his finger around the Bahamas, and Cuba, then way over to Melanesia, then further to Madagascar, then back across to Tahiti, and up to Easter Island as he searched further, and then he just caught sight of them in the corner of his eye — stunned to realise they were only an inch away from where he stood, almost right in front of him. And he turned a little and faced the ocean that way, suddenly wondering about making a quick trip over there before heading up the river, just to sate that old curiosity.

It was only then that the dream made itself more consciously known to him. As Darwin barked in Cladan's ears, images flashbacked across his mind; like on the sides of a coin, the fluttering wings of a knifed flounder bore the profiled faces of his mother's lineage in the Yucatan, as it flapped around dying on the end of his rusty blade.

He suddenly snapped out of it with a shudder, like someone had just tiptoed across his grave. Then he started weighing up the whole point of the trip in any case. He knew it was all just an excuse to escape Melbourne in the end. He always thought he was just going to die there without ever seeing anything else of the world. But gazing over the map again not only made him think of forgoing the river for the Galapagos, but suddenly shifted again at the expense of the islands as well, when he realised just how close he actually was to the land of his ancestors: Mexico was only an inch away, instead of that giant yard from his flat back at home.

The decision was instant.

Though he felt he really had no choice at all, sure it was probably his ma's ghost whispering in his ear to go chase up his indigenous blood all along, as she'd long wished to do herself.

He wondered if he could somehow scalp the Amazon tour back to the agent, or change it around for another package deal instead and continue on. It might give him the unexpected opportunity to fully explore the native region of his forbearers and in the process maybe discover not only who he was, but what he was exactly made of.

Still woozy in the morning, Cladan started ringing around to change the deal. Soon, he was waving off the rest of the party, and scribbling out letters for assistance:

To the Australian Embassy,
Mexico City.

To whom it may concern,
My name is Cladan Kareeda. I am an Australian citizen on holidays in South America, and am considering extending the reach of my travels northerly to Mexico, for less leisurely pursuits: namely I would like to see if I could find some of my ancestors.

My mother, Elli Kareeda (nee Serosa, dec.) was conceived of Mexican blood, and born an Australian citizen in the town of Leongatha in Victoria. She often spoke of her mother, Serisi Serosa (nee Raportia, dec.) who was a citizen of the Yucatan before migrating to Australia as a young woman, whom I never met. (She died just before I was born.) My mother often longed to travel to Mexico and embrace her roots her whole life long, but never did, so I would like to do this, not only for me, but for her, in spirit, as I don't think her ghost would ever rest if I didn't whilst being so close to it on this side of the world.

I plan to make my way to Mexico City over the next week or so via the isthmus, and was hoping by the time I get there you perhaps might be able to help find some record of any of my relatives who might be alive in the Yucatan, who I could finally contact, or perhaps direct me to an institution or agency that might help me there instead. I have enclosed extensive details of my family history — names, dates, migratory patterns and the like. I hope you'll be able to help me, and I'll contact you as soon as I arrive.

Much thanks.

Cladan Kareeda.

PANAMA ➤ Standing on a pier stretched out far into Panama Bay, they all mouthed the word in unison. 1000 pairs of eyes staring out like owls. 1000 breaths in step. The thunderous roll of their impatient fingers tapping along the long white rail at their waists.

They all mouthed the word in unison as they trembled in the chilly winds. It was dusk, and the sun was quickly fizzing in the haze as a dozen chickens swayed off the masts of all the yachts lined up to tempt the Gods; the garfish still bobbing a few abandoned floats; the fat rats scuttling underneath, along the grey rotted beams.

They all mouthed the word in unison as night slowly settled, erasing the horizon. Clusters of stars pinpricked through above, and all the sardines in the creels finally called it a night. The rocking skiffs; the croaking tubs; the stacked boulders to one side covered in moss, shimmering in the moonlight like buffered jade.

They all mouthed the word in unison as the toadies fluttered by. 1000 pairs of hands clutched tightly along the rail. The eyes of statues; cold as bones. The night swamping them all in, including Cladan — still quiet and delirious from the serum — with all the other busloads pulling in to see the sights in the sky as well.

"*Ahora*," they all mouthed together, towards the next sea just out of reach.

Just one leapfrog to go before the world is shucked again.

COSTA RICA ➤ Cladan slowly walked in a daze amongst a long line of tourists lumbering down the centre of the road; each of them following one white line after another, like stepping stones to freer land.

The humidity was stifling. Some were looking off to butterflies flitting by the palm trees dotting the sky, with the cries of flying bananas and macaws in their ears. Others looked to all the Hooker's lips and Blood of Christ flowers dancing to the noon breeze along the sides of the road. Then an old packed-out bus roared by, and all the locals laughed down at them all from the luggage racks in the blinding sun.

Cladan didn't exactly know why he was with them anymore, or where they were all even going, and he could still feel the serum churning in his blood. The hotel had been evacuated because of the second quake, which was even more alarming than the first. But all the tourists had ganged up together outside, and started whining about the heat, the service, the bugs, the cracking walls, and were suddenly all wandering off as a mob in disgust, cursing the shifting earth and everything around them. And now everyone was silent, but still trudging on, just as defiant.

Temptations of paradise were everywhere as they silently filed down the road. Some eyes leered to the right at a few women out in the fields, who were rubbing themselves up against rubber plants to attract luck and men. Then all noses turned left in synch, looking past the coffee bushes to the fields ripe with cane, and out to the pineapple and banana plantations in the distance. Cladan only had a pocketful of granola and smears of peanut butter in waxed paper to cud.

The crowd headed towards the tiny listless town of Zhane, which lay sprawled in the palm of a pocketed valley. Jesus Christ lizards were skimming across all the ponds, and all the black frogs were loudly mooing for miles. A farmer on a tractor hauled plantains past the crowd the other way, but looked back — worried for the lack of smiles. As they all passed the town sign, Cladan loudly announced with a grin, *"We are now all in Zhane."*

But no one laughed.

Everyone remained dour and silent, shuffling along, dripping like taps from the heat. After the quake, jaguars had run amok from out of the woods near town, and were roaming through the nut plantations, still more than rattled. Pickers were on the lookout with pistols, just in case of being stalked in the brush. Some of the locals wandering by looked to the passing crowd like they were some private army out on a drill, but soon decided they were just another gang of foreign twitchers on a spree to snap any bird that moved. To their relief, Costa Rica was still without a force — though the '48 reign of peace had not been in the least recompensed.

When the crowd reached the other end of town, some of the men suddenly broke away and quickly stormed the final store, smashing everything inside, as a few wives carved their initials in the doors. Then they all filed back out onto the road again and caught up with the others, and walked on in silence as before, chewing loose strings of bark from the cinchona trees hanging over the road to ward off the bugs.

Cladan rejoined them a little way ahead again, but loitered back a little towards the rear this time. And then he watched on, stunned, as an eagle carried a screaming howler monkey in its claws across the sky . . .

Passing bungalows on stilts, and towering coconut palms, Cladan followed the crowd as they all veered towards the coast, each of them wavering between potholes in single file like in some old fete game for kids, Cladan thought. Then through heavy scrub and down bamboo steps to the sand, they dragged their feet to the shore, and stood there by the breakers crashing at the edge where, rolling in convulsions, a manatee wildly flapped its fins about, snagged in the shallows, choking on sludge.

Dead baby turtles were floating by in swarms, coughed up by the oily black waves, and screaming gulls trying to peck them out one by one were being mugged in mid-air by frigate birds for the spoils overall.

The crowd gauged the incoming swell for a moment, then disrobed, till they all stood bare as born in a long line along the shore.

Cladan reluctantly peeled himself down to the bones as well.

Then they all held each others hands and entered the water — the ocean creeping up their legs, slapping against their bellies in loud claps — and they kept on walking in as the manatee wriggled to a slump on shore. Then up to their necks, their mouths, their wide staring eyes, they walked in deeper, till they sank beneath the waves; and they walked along the ocean floor, till they hit a reef a little way out, and they climbed up onto the coral and the rocks and went over again, sinking to the bottom again; and they continued to march on, hand in hand, holding their breaths, staying true to their vow of never returning to their hellhole urban lives again where everyone tore at them for nothing but the truth; and they never came back, or surfaced on land again, and just walked on forever.

Or so Cladan dreamt — stuck at the water's edge, with the dead manatee, and all the tiny turtles washing up at his toes.

He was just staring out to the horizon with a frown, subtly covering himself — his legs already bloody from all the chigger bites.

He was wondering if there'd even been a crowd there with him all along.

He felt disorientated, and exhausted, like his mind had just blinked open after it'd been shut down for a spell. And as the sultry squalls returned, eddying the sand, dissolving so much more of it back into the sea, Cladan pondered over all his old long-set doubts about everything that always kept him from ever engaging with anyone who blindly propped themselves up to any cause or principle...

HONDURAS ➤ Cladan was sprawled out flat on his back on a stone altar, on top of the highest Mayan pyramid around, thinking of the thousands of hearts that were once ripped out where he lay. After a while he sat up again, on the top step, and leaned on his knees and rolled a smoke, and soaked up more of the view and the giant blue sky and the stillness that was everywhere around him.

Tourists were wandering around below like ants, looking up at the ruins, but no one else had yet tackled the steep climb of the stairs. He felt cut off up there, away from everyone — the head loner as usual — and had the odd déjà vu sensation of being back home, like nothing had ever changed, as if he'd never budged an inch, and was just sitting alone at a sunny tram stop in St Kilda Road on a Sunday afternoon. But it didn't take long; he soon surrendered himself to daydreaming for a while like he often did when waiting for the 67...

Cladan thought of a gruff American tourist called Gus he'd just bumped into earlier on the way in, and how this Gus had made a huge song and dance about nothing in front of everyone like he was the king of the world. Everyone was amazed to just see him lose it like that, and with his New York accent he looked like he'd stepped straight out of a cop show. Cladan started thinking about Gus as if he was a state military ethicist, sitting in the War Room under the White House, listening to the Joint Chiefs Of Staff discussing the moods of other nations: watching them all playing checkers with Third World countries, chess with Europe, poker with the Middle East. He was middle-aged with receding brown hair, and had a long jagged part cut right between his eyes like the Suez Canal; a salt and pepper beard hugged close to his jaw; tinted BluBlockers on his button-nose; and a bright white shirt holding in a red speckled tie, all tucked neatly inside an inky-blue monkey jacket. Then the Secret Service carried in a cage of white doves and plonked it down onto the huge mapped table of the world in front of them all, smack dab in the middle of the Pacific like a flock of gulls on an atoll. All the little frigates and destroyers, the U-boats and submarines, the minesweepers and aircraft carriers, and all the fleets loaded with amphibious landing crafts, were pulled back to the shores like chips at a casino table. Then the cage was opened — but the birds only cooed, refusing to leave. A four star General soon drew his chrome pistol, and shot it off in the air, and as soft plaster fell from the high ceiling onto the mountains of Canada, all the birds flew out from their enclosure in panic. Then all the other chiefs drew arms as well, and leaned back in their chairs, puffing on stogies, shooting and laughing at every poor bird thudding to the waters of the world without a splash. But Gus only looked on and scribbled a few notes down in a pad, then he got up without a word and quietly left. As a lone motmot called out across the treetops — which transposed in Cladan's ears to a homely wattlebird from home — he dragged on his smoke, imagining the ethicist arriving home from work, and looking straight towards the stuffed head of a shrieking baboon above the mantelpiece as he entered the lounge.

As he headed toward the bar, he brushed away a cobweb newly spun from fang to fang, then prepared himself a Bloody Mary and put on Oscar Peterson, tinkling across the ivories. Above the bar was a stuffed head of a rhino with a tiny porcelain teacup hung off its horn. He dialed a series of numbers on his vintage Crusader Rabbit phone. A vast library bordered the edges of the room, with stacked piles of periodicals in all corners, where his favourite book was stashed — a ragged copy of Green Eggs And Ham with the spine ripped out. "May I speak to his eminence?" he said into the phone, counting out a wad of cash. "My name is irrelevant. Tell him, 'A Messerschmitt is a mosquito designed by committee.' He'll know who it is." He licked a lump of splashed tomato juice off his hand as he waited, then dusted off a plaque hanging above the shot glasses. "Two nuns walk into a bar. Ha. Dandy. Just wanted to confess on the wire. Can't make it in this week. Bless me Father for I have sinned.

*It's been two weeks since my last
confession. I'm still drinking like a
fish, smoking like a chimney, and
swearing like a trooper. Amen. A-
river -dirty. That's Italian for
goodbye. Ha. Bless you back, Padre. "
He hung up and dialed again, biting a
crescent off his pinkie, then reached
up and dropped it into the little China
cup hanging off the horn. "One
supreme," he barked into the phone.
"Double cheese. Thick pan. It's Dr.
Yaal. You've got my address? Okay."
Gus crossed the room and drew the
drapes to a close and flicked on the
box — ad, flicked, ad, flicked it off. He
poured out another Mary at the bar,
picked up the phone, and dialed
again, counting out more cash.
"Giselle's" a woman purred. "Is Livvy
in?" he asked. "When's she on then?
Damn." He slammed down the phone
on the rabbit's hole and stalked off to
the bedroom, then stood on a chair
and unlocked the top cupboard to
remove his doll. But first, before
romancing, he scrubbed his toilet
clean. It's the Catholic thing to do*

before day's end: an old bunker adage he picked up in the last war; a trench habit he just can't seem to shake. And then afterwards, to get to sleep alone, he slowly counted out bushels of beans and barrels of oil to Beethoven's Ode To Joy...

GUATEMALA ➤ By the dying milpa flatlands
of a dribbling river in the heart of nowhere,
Cladan was out looking for the famed White
Nun orchid, and then he stopped to feel the edge
of a dinosaur bone half-buried in the soil, when
suddenly he spotted a cluster of tarantulas
running across the water on their padded feet to
the other side of the valley — and it was only
then that he just happened to notice it.

The air was hot and dead, with the sky
suddenly pocked like a cork. Upstream, a family
washing clothes on the rocks stopped as well on
spotting it.

Adobe huts lay scattered everywhere in
the distance, and everyone was stepping
outside to see what was going on, shielding
their eyes from the sun — the prayer leaders
letting loose great wafts of incense from their
robes as they appeared, stoic and composed.

The village women sipping cocoa in
colourful tunics sat transfixed in the shade,
watching on dumb the same. Other women
with pots on their heads stood silent in groups,
eyes wide, their mouths just holes.

Most of the men, in ragged denim,
chewing chicle, and gobbing, only watched on
with tears in their eyes. Old luggers with loads

of water jugs on their backs froze in their tracks on seeing it as well.

No one left the area. It was all too clear to Cladan to simply stay on and watch it as well. Elderly couples huddled close by on wooden staffs, gazing in awe, reavowing old oaths long compromised in their youth.

Then two women collapsed, overwhelmed, and an old mule starved down to the ribs ran away in fear. Kids stood still and strong with squirming quetzals in their arms, staring on in palpable glee.

There was no trouble anywhere, even though a civil patrol quietly arrived to control things. But once they saw it as well, they didn't even bother with their typical ways of rule. They knew all the answers too, soon as they saw it, just like everyone else did.

No one let the few more than obvious tourists within range. They tried hard to get through with their cameras, but the locals formed the tightest cage with their shoulders, their hands linked together like chains in the air to keep them all at bay.

Time suddenly seemed stilled awhile, as if deactivated, yet it retained everything so comfortably, that the impingement of evening had no effect at all.

Cladan hadn't moved from his spot a single step for hours, and pleasantly watched the day turn to night, not caring anymore why no one else had budged an inch around him either. He thought he'd be there forever and quite preferred the idea because everyone seemed so strangely buoyant.

People held flaming torches high and began to sing in little clans here and there about the *"Popol Vuh,"* sipping at cups of ayahuasca. Some broke out animal masks and started wild dances. Flutes were soon ringing the air; bean gourds rattling. Others wheeled out idols of saints and held them high above the heads of everyone to bless the sight. A few clutched tiny carved statuettes to their chests in prayer.

Then a woman who appeared jealous suddenly attacked another. Then a tourist playfully stroked a doll tied to the back of a little girl, who screamed, and a scrum of men began to beat into him like madmen.

"You filch our spawn for their insides!" every mother screamed, clutching their children to their skirts.

Then, out of nowhere, soldiers suddenly appeared out of every cranny, moving in on everyone, pushing and shoving their way through. And then someone stabbed one of their horses, and all the other horses reared up wild and charged through the crowd, trampling two children to death.

A few old villagers weakly threw hollow painted eggs filled with confetti at them all — their only munition. Then the youngest soldiers began to club people indiscriminately, and guns were firing off, and everyone was suddenly scattering everywhere, screaming through the lots, blood spilt all over the dusty paths.

Cladan raced off too, with his new party, shooting down a muddy alleyway. Suddenly everyone was back inside their huts, full of fear, treating their wounds, taking back all their promises . . .

Early the next morning, everyone ran out into the open air. All the blood was still sticky on the earth, swarming with earwigs and thrips — the damage untouched.

Everyone, including Cladan, was asking everyone else in guarded whispers, what was that thing they all saw together?

MEXICO ➤ The embassy official tilted back in his high-backed chair, with his hands locked behind his head, and laughed his guts out at Cladan sitting across the desk from him: speckles of his spit glistening in the window light like a sudden cosmos.

Cladan just stared back blankly at him, weary for meeting one of his countrymen — he'd made a vow to immediately steer himself away if ever bumping into any one of them on his trip. But now, stuck with this flunky, the surly way he talked down to him like he was nothing, the snide way he regarded him like he had all the power in the world and knew it, made Cladan feel an old fire reignite in himself, and these embers that quickly caught alight lit up the side of him that he hated, because this was the side that hated himself, and he knew sometimes that old fire could run amok in no time and razz everything inside himself before the day was done.

"Look, Mr. Kary-da," the official said, mispronouncing his name, *"you have to admit, it's outlandish."* He leaned forward, picking up Cladan's letter, and waved it about. *"We cannot do your family tree."*

Cladan felt like he was back home again on just hearing the official's voice, and then he started loathing the sound of his own as well, with every word he said back himself.

"I thought you'd just hit a button," Cladan stammered, *"and someone does a quick run on a little data for a citizen who's over here, and you know, something like this just gets done. Like a service, payed by our taxes."*

With a dead smile, the official dropped the letter on Cladan's side of the desk, and said, *"This button does not exist."*

Cladan picked up his letter and folded it and put it in his shirt-pocket, staring at the floor in thought for a moment. It was clear to him he was allowed a moment to think. The official leaned back in his chair again.

"Who should I see then?" Cladan said, looking back at him.

"A genealogist?" the official replied in a rising lilt, his eyebrows disappearing somewhere in his hair.

Cladan just stared back sourly at him, feeling a sort of bile rising inside himself.

"Try a phone book," the official snapped. *"Head to the Vatican, I mean the Yucatan, and look up any Serosa's in the phone book, and go from there."*

Soon as Cladan pushed open the heavy embassy door and stepped back outside,

Mexico City hit him hard and fast like a punch in the face. Traffic flying by. Brakes screeching. Horns blaring. People packed in like sardines for as far as he could see. The stench alone nearly rocked his knees. Lying dead in the gutter by a nearby scrum of midget clowns cleaning windscreens lay the twisted remains of a skinny black dog without eyes, ants teeming all over it. Though its initial stink didn't stand a chance to get past the general reek of everything else already drowning out his thoughts.

Then a squirming pig tied around the shoulders of a passing motorcyclist moved by him at eye level and vomited in his face. And this was the moment that suddenly ruined everything for him there. He turned to a middle-aged man in a suit walking down the street, his face cut in half by a huge moustache.

"Excuse me," Cladan said in a flustered tone, wiping vomit from his face, and was just about to ask where the Post Office was, when the man suddenly flinched.

"I am not your lover!" he screamed back, storming on ahead. *"Rape your mother! Go to the fucked!"*

Cladan just froze in his tracks.

It was like something inside him had just crystallized, and broken off, disappearing into a chasm without a sound.

He couldn't walk on for a moment, and thought about just sitting down somewhere for a second, but the immediate thing he felt compelled to do was retreat.

Sitting in a daze on a park bench, Cladan watched a band of mariachis busking under the twisted shade of a colossal frangipani tree. Families were gathered everywhere under its giant shadow watching a troupe in costumes do their cultural worst. Dancers were decked out in old burlap sacks and palm-leaved coats, with strings of cocoons swinging about their necks and waists. People in half-masks and fake beards were charging paper mache bulls at kids dressed as snarling jaguars, and everybody was cheering them on.

Cladan swigged down mouthfuls of mezcal from a lemonade bottle like he used to do with Bourbon in a coke can at the drive-in when he was a teenager with friends. With each mouthful he downed, he felt like he was dissolving himself bit by bit, and was glad for the relief of it. But after a while, the festivities blurred into a riot of noise that no longer interested him anymore. He felt suddenly self-conscious about what a local had just screamed at him, paranoid that every eye was now glued to him in the same way.

Was it because he was a gringo? he wondered. Or was it his clothes? They weren't inordinately fashionable by a long shot. Or was it his ratty hair? Or was it the old dreaded baby face — courtesy of all the spoonfuls of molasses he'd obediently downed as a boy at the hands of his pop, who drilled in him to never change his expression when he swallowed?

Cladan looked at all the men in the crowd, wondering if he appeared odd or effeminate in comparison, and soon came to the conclusion that he could no longer communicate any further in Mexico until he grew a substantial moustache like everyone else.

The old concierge staggered down the grimy corridor, chattering Spanish to her adult son, who sullenly followed, gorging on a tortilla, as they led Cladan on to see the room. The son could only speak a butchered English himself, and was the only conduit to bridge Cladan's inquiries about the room to his mother. Even then, the son had some problems with Cladan's accent. Initially, everywhere he went it seemed, Cladan was automatically deemed an American — until he spoke.

The room was a basic bed-sit, about the size of a garden shed. Old red paint was peeling off the windowsill and the door, and narrow strips of wallpaper covered in tiny watermelons had been torn away from its edges here and there every arm-length, with little strange circular markings everywhere. The single bed was neatly made, and across the border of the sheet, folded over what looked like an old horse blanket, was the name "PAQUA MOTEL" in faded blue copperplate that looked like it'd been washed a thousand times. Above the bed hung a plastic framed icon of the Madonna: her burnt-out eyes twinkling white as stars.

The son then opened the closet and removed what at first appeared to be a mop or a broom, but attached at one end was a vegetable-chopper on a spring. He explained to Cladan in more gestures than words that it was for the tarantulas. Cladan could feel the hairs rising on his neck like charged nettles in a field before a storm at the sheer mention of this. To explain how it worked, the son tore a corner of his tortilla off and dropped it on the floor, then housed the contraption over it, and after a few quick pumps, moved it away in a flash, proudly revealing a small pile of mangled shreds.

Bug-eyed, Cladan looked to the concierge, who, on making eye contact with him, robotically stuck out her hand to be paid. Almost as if he had no will of his own, he forked out the cash, and they both darted out of the room, leaving him standing there, holding the chopper in his hands, as he slowly scanned the walls for anything that might suddenly move of its own accord, listening to them cackling with laughter down the stairway. But he knew there'd be only one way he'd ever lie down in that ratty bed, and that would be drunk.

Cladan was soon sitting in a corner of a nearby club, watching a brass combo do its worst up on stage down the other end. Half the crowd stood at the feet of the band, punching fists in the air.

The other half was over at the bar, tossing back shots, counting down with every round, *"Arriba! Abayo! Al centro! Adento!"*

Then everyone went *"Salud"* everywhere till the whole place trilled like it was walled with doves.

Cladan had tunneled his way through to
the bar and back a few times for a beer, and
watched the band up close for a while, but
soon pulled back, and was leaning on a table
at the rear, with a jug of beer in front of him,
and a hand over his mouth as he scribbled on
the back of a coaster.

1. Gro mo.
2. Go to PO, 4 Yuc Pho·bks.
3. Truk to Yuc.

He guzzled on his beer, wondering about
the huge expanse of the Yucatan, and whether
his ancestors might still be out there in force.
Maybe the peninsula was teeming with them?
He could feel it drawing him towards it. As the
music soared, he thought about the province of
Quintana Roo he kept on hearing about all
day, which blipped his radar.

Possible obvious expat enclave? he
wondered.

4. Str8 thru Roo.

As the band took a welcome break,
everyone rushed back to the bar in droves. Some
staggered laughing towards the amenities, and
others back up to the pool tables down the other

end. Soon, Cladan's table was scooped up in the rush, and two men and a woman were suddenly seated with him, watching another woman rack up a table for a game. They were all yelling in Spanish and laughing their heads off like everyone else as a tiny cue stick the size of a candy cane was offered to one of the men, who jumped up from his seat and took his shot as the woman who'd just broke sat down and asked a waiter for a pulque.

Then the jukebox was blaring, and people were moving about everywhere again, loading up at the bar in the break — the players swapping seats, swapping shots.

After what had happened earlier in the day, Cladan felt shy and didn't feel like talking to anyone, and was sitting on his last beer, and was about to go, when they suddenly invited him to join a game as one of the men headed back to the band stepping out on stage again.

After a time, the five of them were soon over at the bar having a tequila contest like everyone else stretched all the way down to the other end. Cladan couldn't stop staring at a large granite idol propped on the counter. It looked ancient, and flawlessly formed: a figure holding a carved bowl in its hands, full with water, and strips of cactus floating inside.

The girlfriend of one of the men pointed out to him how Mayans used to drink the raw juices out of maguey plants in rituals to connect with other worlds.

"It used to make them dip their eyes into the stars for a while, to help spread everything out a bit," she said in clipped English, *"till time became more a tool, than just a counterweight."*

Then they all started a chili game tied in with the tequila duels, and bowls of the hottest and reddest came out from under the bar.

People were daring one another to head off to The Liver Does Not Exist, to finally swallow the famed Crying Tongue. But soon, Cladan couldn't see or hear anything anymore, and they were all falling over each other drunk, and laughing their heads off like everyone else as the band did their final set.

Someone soon floated the idea of getting maguey from a nearby plantation, and all Cladan knew was he was standing in the back of a jeep with everyone else, and clinging to a roll cage as they roared across the desert in the dark, with the wind in his face, the stars everywhere, and everyone screaming drunk and happy.

One of the men hanging on to the cage pointed out something in the headlights.

"Two rabbits!" he yelled, looking back, amazed, like it was a sign of luck, and he kept on pointing off and cheering as his girlfriend hung on to him.

Everyone else cheered him on as well, patting him on the back, saying it was a blessing to see, that he'd live a wise and lucky life.

His girlfriend turned to Cladan and loudly explained.

"Two Rabbits is the Aztec God of Wine. He had 400 sons!"

"Is that why he was called rabbit?" Cladan asked out loud in the racket.

But they all just laughed, and the jeep soon pulled up to the edge of a vast plateau where there was enough clear moonlight reflected across the maguey plants below to give the valley the illusion of a rocky inbound sea.

Squatted on her haunches at the root of a towering plant, the girlfriend sliced off a wide thorny arm with a knife, and divvied it up, then scored the edges of each portion she handed out to everyone.

Cladan was soon sucking the juices out of each cut like everyone else, with his nose running loose, and his eyes wobbling wild, as he staggered about drunk on the spot.

"G-i-l-a!" he roared up at the sky, like he was calling out for a reply.

Everyone burst out laughing at the strange way he blinked as he listened intently to his echo bouncing around the huge silent valley.

"When I found out the Gila Monster and the Mexican Beaded lizard were the only poisonous lizards in the world," Cladan slurred, wavering on his feet, stepping back two steps and then forward again, *"it was like this big secret to me as a kid. I never told anyone. No one knew."*

"Apaches say if one breathes on you, you will die."

"The Tohono say they're spiritual guides."

Initially, Cladan felt like his throat was on fire from all the chili and tequila; but now it was as if it was all suddenly hairy and rancid, and chewed out by worms like the rotted throat of a dragon, and he was parched. Then two of the men plucked peyote out of the ground like they were picking up dropped buttons. Soon, Cladan's vision fractured like a kaleidoscope, splintering everything he saw into a dozen plying selves, as if barely anything was held together by a common grain. He felt like he was upside-down, and falling. Then his knees went under him, and he dropped back to the earth, landing on his back, and he stared up at the stars scattered everywhere across the clear sky, and he could hear the others chuckling. But he felt happy, and he suddenly sang a song he couldn't sing fast enough to keep them married:

> *"You wouldn't know Mao*
> *from a Hindu cow,*
> *you wouldn't know God*
> *from a dog.*
> *You wouldn't know Buddha*
> *from a woodworm, would you,*
> *if you could now,*
> *and you couldn't bow down?*
>
> *You wouldn't know fun*
> *from a milking gun,*
> *you wouldn't know wit*
> *from a quack.*
> *You wouldn't know love*
> *from a mouthful of mud,*
> *you wouldn't know now,*
> *would you, how?"*

As the others laughed out loud, Cladan was surprised at how joyous he suddenly felt, but at the same time he also felt a sudden subtle wave of homesickness washing through him as he stared up at the sky. Dangling to one side of his face was the end of a maguey arm. It seemed like each thorn around its edge had snared a star, and he could feel his eyes reigniting with every twinkle as he spotted each one of them. He could feel different parts of his body being pinned to the earth by the sting of each separate sun, like there were as many bits of him as there were of them. Suddenly he announced that he felt compelled to sing the unofficial national anthem of his homeland. And they all joined in after they asked him to repeat it again, and sang it solemnly, and heartedly, in echoes across the valley, as Cladan slowly passed out...

"We are dumb,
and we are scar-y,
and the flies
buzz around us
the size of dogs.

We share a scream,
and stink like high hogs!
Fuck-en hu-mans.
We are a pack o' cunts."

As sunlight broke out in broad streaks across the morning sky, the weird yawp of something scuttling through the scrub suddenly woke Cladan, and he bolted up from his sleep, tearing a cheek open across the end of the hanging maguey arm. Blood trickled down his face like a line of tears, as if a new eye had just opened up, wept, and shut again, and it all crawled down his neck as the sun inched up the sky behind him.

His head was grinding like stone on stone.

His eyes felt like they were tied to the busted arse of an ass on it's bended way down through the fiery hills of Hell.

The valley was empty for as far as he could see: the jeep and his Mexican friends nowhere.

Instinctively, he clutched at his waist: his shirt was open and the money belt gone.

He wandered about in a daze, wondering where the hell he was, looking around at the desolate landscape, dreading the silence, feeling the heat already rising in the earth, and with all of the cacti towering tall as trees everywhere, he felt as alone as if he was abandoned on Mars.

Then he tripped, and tumbled over into a crevice, plummeting metres down into a ditch full of skunks, who all hissed and screeched and clawed and sprayed at him with everything they had.

Within hours, a guide leading a crowd of tourists through the scrub discovered him, and he was rushed off to a hospital in Mexico City. He was semi-conscious, and — in accordance with his insurance — put straight on an ambulance jet, and sent flying back home across the Pacific.

A nurse seated beside him cupped her face with an oxygen mask to block out the relentless pong as he mumbled to himself the whole way. He had a cracked pelvis and a cactus in his heart.

TRANSCRIPT
(FOR INSURANCE PURPOSES ONLY)
EXCERPTS OF PATIENT'S RECORDED
VERBIAGE IN TRANSIT:

"...we'd just huddle inside... those old greying days... listening to the sky... staring in her eyes... rising from our desks... level with her face ...and we'd vanish for hours... out of harm's way... She threw dust at us later... and we slowly reappeared... drifting down again... basking in the rays...

*through the panes... the bay wind
retreating... and we'd re-gather
ourselves... But what was left...
drifted out the door... worming up for
the next dawn... no matter what all
the prayers were for..."*

+ 9 hrs. (etc.)

SUMMARY:
SOP delirium.
Gibberish.
Irrelevant.

26

MAN WITHOUT A TONGUE
AND THE WOMEN
WHO LOVED HIM

Cladan was still nostril-laughing to himself as he headed back through the kitchens to delicately wrap Fintonia's wrist in ice and listen to her secret stories again. One was about how she'd accidentally chopped off the tip of one of her pinkies into a cake mix when she was a kid and fed it to her foster-ma anyway, the same night she'd glued her foster-pa's beard to his pillow, and how he nearly suffocated himself in his sleep.

Fintonia was short, but with the giant coffee eyes of a giraffe; her long lashes gently batting on her cheeks like fronds as she blinked.

She was seven years younger than Cladan to the day, and was living back with her birth parents for a while. She told him about how her parents once ran a tiny post office in a village in the Wimmera when she was born, and how they'd change her on the counter, weighing up the nappies, laughing their heads off; but soon the locals complained about the smell, so they did it out the back amongst the mail. Then all the postmen gave them a serve for having to deal out all these stinking slices of shit all over town to everyone. It was around that time her godmother was strangled by the town baker. Her neighbour, Mrs. Riverrot, had heard the kettle whistling for an hour or more, so she nicked over the fence and found her in the laundry — dead blue, eyes popped to burst, with fingerprints in flour right round her throat. Fintonia said the locals always said *"the baker was a few slices short of the loaf, but he made the most beautiful bread." "Hands of a pianist,"* they all said. And *"all the kids at school always ate their crusts."*

Cladan tried tying the napkin hard as he giggled, but his rubber gloves were wet and he was scared he'd hurt her sprained wrist. Fintonia blamed her clumsiness on all her *"inherited stuff",* on account of having a *"Mexican jumping-bean type-mind."*

Cladan hadn't told her of his heritage, and asked her where she got that line.

"TV," she reluctantly admitted, as she looked at him a little shyly, then looked away. *"Don Rickles, I think."*

Then she started on another story about how her fisherman cousin had two navels and burst into flames in his sleep — but their boss, Vicki, suddenly stepped back in from the market, and Fintonia darted back to the tables, and Cladan went back to the pit and resumed the drudgery.

"No one's eating the birds," Vicki seethed to Pini, tipping them all into the bin.

Pini looked up, hung-over, as she cookie-cutted pastry sheets into pies, and quietly confirmed the same. *"Not one."*

Vicki used to drown them out the back, before the inspector found out. That was in the good old days when she first started up and all the butchers caved in to the competition: poultry was sweeping the world then, on account of all the mad cow disease. But now the bird flu scare had everyone reeling.

Vicki always played the boss, but she was no monster. She'd call everyone *"darl,"* and whenever she laughed she'd always turn around and do it right in a person's face like she knew who she was. She seemed to lead a very full life. Whereas Cladan only pretended to, and at heart knew he was never a success at fooling anyone. He was only full of second-hand news all the time. But no one knew he was seeing a counselor — a jaded Madagascan would scribble down all the poisons he spat across his desk each Tuesday a.m. But Cladan was beginning to doubt the point of it all anymore. It all felt like a waste of time. And anyway, his deadline was coming up.

As he scrubbed away, he started thinking in hindsight again, like all the other times before, dreaming of how he should've gently kissed Fintonia's wrist and said it was *"for medicinal purposes,"* or *"help with the healing,"* or something like that. He thought maybe that would've made her see him in a different light — but he didn't do it, because he thought it probably wouldn't come off all that clean in the end. Maybe in theory, but sober, he knew soon as he ever gave those ones a bit of air, onto the block they'd go, and whack! head to the left, guts to the right, next! It always came out like some dead thing on TV. Like he just did the worst thing when he meant to do his best. He sees romance as dead now anyway, and glad of it. As he scoured out all the pans, he went over the graph he'd just spotted in the paper, listing all that had unfolded so far ...

1.   Big bang.
2.   Earth.
3.   Life.
4.   Vertebrates.
5.   Primates.
6.   Hominisation.
7.   Homo Sapiens.
8.   Agriculture.
9.   The Sumerian civilisation.
10. Buddha.
11. Christ.
12. Mohammed.
13. The Renaissance.
14. World economy.
15. The Industrial Revolution
16. Modern science and art.
17. Atomic energy.
18. Computers.

Thirteen billion years worth, he pondered, over the trillions of bubbles in the suds.

But Fintonia suddenly rushed in, saying she'd just served a Buddhist tea and he'd revealed to her the four basic truths, plus the Noble Eightfold Path.

1. Life is fundamentally disappointment and suffering.

2. Suffering is a result of one's desires for pleasure, power, and continued existence.

3. To stop disappointment and suffering, one must stop desiring.

4. The way to stop desiring, and thus suffering, is the Noble Eightfold Path:

   1) Right views
   2) Intentions
   3) Speech
   4) Conduct
   5) Livelihood
   6) Effort
   7) Mindfulness
   8) Concentration

Then they heard the big news over the radio that astronomers had just discovered a galaxy wall 500 million light years long, 200 million light years wide, and 20 million light years thick, and described it as *"Possibly the white picket fence around God's front yard. We know where He is now."*

Vicki walked through, and they both stopped her in her tracks and told her and Pini out in the shop. Vicki couldn't believe it, and hugged them all, then shut up the shop for the afternoon to celebrate, breaking out champagne and black forest cake, and everyone just laughed and cheered and toasted to everything in the world for the rest of the day.

Hmm, Cladan thought — reconsidering everything — *maybe it's worth postponing next month's note. Something might finally be happening.*

27
A CUT ABOVE
THE ~~REST~~ WRIST

Adouble-semi loaded with shipping containers coasted down the promenade hugging the shore, decelerating loudly as it rounded the bend, rattling all the glasses in the tavern, briefly drowning out the jukebox and all the bleeps and bloops of the pokies, but not a pensioner flinched as they kept on slotting coins in a trance like a pack of chimps.

"Sheer fugacity, my friend," the hefty bald doorman quipped to his burly offsider as Cladan walked drunk out the door. *"Sheer,"* he repeated with raised eyebrows.

"F" Chrissakes," Cladan slurred to himself as he stepped outside into the icy sea wind, looking up sourly at the fading sunshine — all the gunmetal clouds were rolling back in again like they had for days on end.

"Fuckassity?" he asked himself, as he wavered across the bend in the road, sniggering.

But a thousand other more pressing thoughts were scrambling through his mind as well, and he wandered over to a park near the beach, and slumped down on a bench seat by an old cenotaph towering by Flip Bay, his hair blowing over his face as he tried to roll a smoke from the dregs in his pack.

"Twenty times the circumference of the earth we plod, and for what?" he growled out loud in a different voice, mimicking someone from the bar.

"That's what he said!" he said back to himself in the same agitated way he overheard the reply. Then he repeated it again as he tried to light up, shaking his lighter about, and he chuckled half-heartedly in a desperate attempt to cheer himself up, but he knew nothing could ever work.

"Mysticism... plus masochism... equals Catholicism," he slurred to himself, imitating someone else he overheard, desperate to make himself laugh again. *"Mister Cism? Whozat?"*

He lifted a leg up and held onto his knee to keep warm from the hard bay winds ricocheting off the cliff into his face, and he dragged on his smoke, thinking of how he'd just palmed off Fintonia to the hack in the street behind the tavern for the night *"to be fixed,"* — as she put it. She must've been just as drunk as him as they parted.

"Seventeen's the new twenty," he slurred. *"They gild the lily. Every one."*

He looked up at the grey clouds bunching under themselves for an almighty crack.

"Where were they all... before they all became?" he mumbled to himself — tears crashing out of his eyes as he stared out across the choppy sea.

His face was already freezing as he tried lighting his smoke again. There wasn't a soul around, and the filthy bay looked like a sewerage farm after the week's relentless rains, churning over and over like his guts.

"Everyone appearing, and disappearing," he grumbled. *"Taking over everything again."* And he tried to talk further, but he kept on hiccupping. *"The hearts... the eyes... this fucking home of the dead."*

Suddenly he blubbered, and bent over, he quickly stumbled away from the seat and collapsed behind the shrubs to one side like a dying boar, to crash the night there, so he could fetch Fintonia first thing in the morning.

Soon, he was heaving his guts out to one side, till he fell on his back again, drained and miserable and frozen.

"Lest we forget the mourners hum forever hymned," he recited, trying to read the epitaph chiseled deep into the cenotaph through the leaves.

The relentless winds shook all the salt bushes about like they were rattles, though he welcomed the racket of it all, with the sea crashing in back of him, and all the wind's whirrs as well — anything to help block out his nagging thoughts — and he slowly fell asleep beneath the ferns, just out of view of anyone who might pass along the track. The dread, gently fading as he slept, fully stored to return with all the other larks in his mind chewing at his life already. That, and his constipated squeeze, squatted across the way, losing both bundles down the chute.

28
PUBLICIANA

Cladan tossed back a final shot in the local bar, zipped his jacket up, then stepped out of the liquor shop with a boxed bottle of grenadine under his arm and headed off to meet Fintonia at her parents' house for dinner for the first time. But just as he stepped off the curb in the rain, the side mirror of a van suddenly slapped his face as it turned the corner, knocking him flat, and he rolled back down into the runny gutter like a dropped pipe.

People ran over to him under umbrellas — as did the driver, who'd blocked off traffic as he pulled up hard in the middle of the turn and rushed back — but Cladan was in a daze and didn't realise what had exactly happened, and for a moment he could barely see or hear anything, with the rain pelting down on his face, and he could feel all the slosh flowing down the gutter down his back, and the quick cold shook his blood and chattered his teeth as his vision began to cloud.

"Shit, no," the driver whimpered on seeing him sprawled there, white as a ghost, and he quickly crouched down to him. *"Can you move?"*

Cladan squinted, blinking, under the shadow of the High Commission Flats across the road, only to see wedged high in all the floors above him, the lonely glowing eyes of tenants staring down orange at him like hovering wasps. Their troubled thoughts dropped down like plumb bobs, dangling in his face, and nipped at his ears in crazy tongues. Then a weather-beaten stretch from the bar barked out loud for an ambulance as assorted tribes looked Cladan over: businessmen, winos, shoppers, and punks. Passing mobs shaking down their heads at him like sheep.

The driver leaned over Cladan's face to block out the sudden hail and meekly peeked into the faint fizzle of ions arcing beneath his lids.

"Sit tight, mate," he groaned, getting hammered in the downpour, and he looked up to the crowd huddled close by under shelter, all of them staring at him.

"He jumped out right in front of me!" he implored to them all.

Through Cladan's eyes, everything was becoming fuzzy. His eyelids slamming like hammers. Each blink a mirror of the chaos of his life long percolated in his mind over the years, all of it staled and stifled. But the hurts and injustices he'd coldly absorbed over the years no longer bruised his nerves, or burst into rashes, or whitened his hair. It'd seeped through the bones like radiation now, spiking the marrow, and like an icy pole sucked clear he pulsated an incandescent reptile glow.

After a while a soaked dog tied to a post outside the pub door howled out loud for a chance to be freed as people hailed down taxis in the rain to get home and collapse themselves. And those few left behind soon cleared themselves away as the paramedics knelt over Cladan, pinching his knees and bending his elbows.

"He's a leaper!" the driver kept on gabbling in their ears. *"A friggin' roo!"*

Cladan was soon whisked away to the DSH holding ward of the Melbourne Remand Asylum, where self-saboteurs lay scattered about in their high chromed cots everywhere, hypnotised by the TVs fizzing above them like Aspros.

Belted down, Cladan watched on too, till he felt the spluttering of the light slowly baking his eyes to scones. Then his arms cracked at the pits, his legs at the groin, his face at the chin, and as his nose dropped away like clay, his bones began to quake, till his flesh fell away in tumbling sheaves, leaving just a bare, pink, sticky thing of a grub with trembling fingers like worms. He could feel everything welling up within him like a shook can of Coke about to pop. The side-streets of his bloodshot eyes untangling like golf balls at the seams, unraveling a million rotten memories; old faces of friends flickering by like fireflies with the dead look of dolls; old street signs of his youth slapping his cheeks like insulted hosts...

A sliver of light gently threaded Cladan's eyes as he emerged in a drip-dry neon morning, with breakfast hanging over his bed like a bat. Cold toast like cardboard with a cowpat clump of scrambled eggs, all drowned in a beige hollandaise sauce the consistency of spit. And to wash it all down, a stained plastic toy cup full of cold slop the colour of bile. He pushed the trolley away, trying to block out the stench of vomit clouding the ward as the nurses wandered about changing pans and sheets.

A priest on crutches zigzagged ward to ward, nodding to the self-gassed across the way, who all barked out hoarse for ice cream from inside their tents. To one side, a clumping cripple on a corked hoof slowly moved by like a ship of the desert, as a fat gangster under anesthetic in the corner mumbled platitudes regarding his wife's remarkable vulva. Drips in every arm; charts at every ankle like amulets. Patients faced the windows for hours like they were eyeing off an old master's view of paradise. On the horizon, a lone pier stuck out loosely across Flip Bay like a breadknife. A curved black slash of road lashed the coast like a line of mascara. The shimmering rays of the sun lighting up the sea like petrol flames.

Close by, on a dangling leaf by a window, Cladan spotted the reflecting dots on a ladybird's back glistening in the sunlight like a digital watch.

"7:12? Is it 7:12?" he said aloud, or in his head, he wasn't sure.

In the next bed, a bald man, up to his wrists in pilliwinks, spat smithereens of his rotten life into Cladan's clammy ear. His father reprimanded his sense of worth, whittled him down to his soul, and then played the bagpipes in his face as he jigged around his heart. He'd tried to hang himself with a fishing line and nearly circumcised his head. He had 36 stitches in the throat and a voice like a Komodo dragon. His eyes like rusted roofing nails holding on the scalp.

Then, like a ventriloquist without the dummy, death's mule trotted by, nibbling at a vase of roses in the corridor. Cladan spotted it's blue pillow lips crunching at petals like chips, spitting thorns out like pips, and like spinning ninja-stars they fixed sturdy to the doorway like a halo, illuminating the long winding track leading back to the outside world, where everyone's deranged from day one by a universal gang bent on greed, hate and revenge to become the same; a mindless slave who'll lap like a dog for a meagre reward; a hopeless slob hooked on vengeance; a blood-brother of the mob; a eunuch forever chained to the grave.

As night fell again, the matron, swathed in a marmot stole, clacked down the hall in her stilettos, with her tiny hobnailed heels echoing like cap guns. Drugged-out wrecks lay scattered around the wards on slabs everywhere, wheezing like bagpipes, prattling on like chooks in their sleep. Some knee-deep in dreams, their faces morphing into gargoyles. All of them twitching about like beached whales moaning in a chorus. Noses inhaling into garlands. Mouths metamorphosing into jam jars. Monsters yawning cute as pups, as the rag and bone widows slowly creaked in their throats like rotted stairs. A comatose band of dum-dums spraying rind galaxies in bright orange clusters, all tucked in a whitewashed corral, chanting zzz's to the pulse of the million drops slowly drowning them.

Yep, Cladan thought — sighing out loud in the racket — *we ossify early, till we're all palatable to the taste. We're either trained to be sceptic merchants or hara-kiri instructors, palming off the same old shucked seed shore to shore like plagues of starfish inoculating reefs with dropsy. And like peppered hogs, everyone lies in wait, begging for the steel at the end.*

But on his second morning there, the nurses handed him a bottle of iron tablets and kicked him out. *"You're on the verge of anaemia. Eat properly. Try broccoli, or a carrot for once in your life,"* someone hollered out after him as he wandered off into the sunshine.

He was suddenly clean, and freshly shaved, and though he felt slightly wonky, he continued on — as if uninterrupted —

resuming his journey to Fintonia's parents' house, where they'd expected him for dinner two nights before. Thought they might have him for lunch instead.

Half a dozen cars were parked up the double driveway, and the front door was as wide open as the sky. Cladan knocked, but there was no answer, so he cautiously entered.

The lounge-room was littered with coats and bags and kids' toys, and in the air swirled a faint waft of butane gas. He caught sight of a long single waving red hair poking out from a wall in the kitchen, and walked over to it, eyes glued. It was caught on a dog magnet in the sunlight, anchoring a note to the fridge with Fintonia's mother's shopping list nearly all ticked off.

Cladan stepped out into the sunny backyard to find Fintonia with a crowd of her relatives having a barbecue. And he quickly fobbed off the last few days absence as an unexpected family misadventure, without elaborating — winking at her, meaning he'd tell her later — and joined in with everyone else as she introduced him around, though he sensed immediately that her parents detested him. But the smell of all the fresh food almost threw him. The lamb chops, sizzling brown, tasted so rich and succulent in the midday sun after the last few days retching in hospital. The sausages crunched crisp and hearty with the old age black dew flavour of a million barbies long gone before him. Lettuce was sparkling everywhere in the sunshine, and a bloody bowl of sliced beetroot glistened under the blue sky like the petals of a giant rose.

Everything was sweet. Fintonia's auntie was a loud and crazy lady, full of the pure unadorned love of life Cladan wished his own stock had. She laughed so loud and infectiously, a neighbour peeked over a fence — curious of the catalyst. Her new husband was the same, full of life, even though he only had one leg, but all he talked about was the sea and his old faithful tugboat, Dympna — occasionally throwing in the odd reference to 'Nam. Cladan assumed he'd stepped on a mine. His wife's excuse wasn't so evident.

Fintonia's parents were less charming — but in a more obtrusive way — infantile beyond words. Her ma constantly cried to get attention, blaming the smoke from the barbie, even though the wind was blowing the other way, and continually made guarded comments to guests regarding a certain He, but never by name.

Fintonia's pop was a fat gregarious man in a chef's hat, with G'DAY printed above his brow, who wore a burnt apron with a pair of tits and a cunt emblazed. And across his face — a large nearly toothless grin. The one eyebrow across the raisins really underlined the whole thing. And all he talked about was the cooking; how various gristles were different, and the acoustics of fat and the properties therein. How there was a fundamental contrast between the sinew and the tendon when the rubber hit the road. How the musical cackle of the grill differed between grades of flesh. How the raw waste of the sausage barked obscenities, whereas the steak tended to hum and sing. Even the eggs received a serve. He never once referred to anything else other than what they were about to receive, and gave every indication that if ever that line was crossed, he would immediately vanish to bed in a shit.

Fintonia sat by Cladan again, with a hand on his leg under the table, as he greedily devoured everything slapped onto his paper plate. He wolfed down the bread Fintonia's ma buttered so fast that she couldn't keep up with him as he made small talk with everyone else — mopping up puddles of sauce, swabbing the plate clean, slice after slice. And all the while her ma kept on asking if he wanted more, and Cladan kept on nodding to keep them coming, gulping at his beer, scooping at the coleslaw, forking more sausages; and she was straining her fingers to butter the bread, just to keep up — and inside, Cladan's guts were busting with laughter because he knew he was in front. And that's when it all really gelled.

Fintonia's parents knew Cladan wasn't impressed with them at all. They knew he didn't care about their nifty ways with the outdoors, or their three storey house, or their double garage with the Merc and the Jag. They knew he didn't give a toss about their lavish bar, or the baby grand, or their vintage wines, or their mangy wolf Ranga. They knew he loathed them just as much as they loathed him. They knew their measly suburban ways grated on his nerves, and the fact that he smiled like a criminal in their own backyard, whilst chomping on their steaks, sucking on their bones, and making faces at their guests — and knowing that all he wanted was their daughter in the end — quietly infuriated them. Especially after guzzling all the beer he could find, and stripping down and swimming in the pool with Fintonia; then dripping all over them, raving drunk as a loon, and watching her lapping it all up.

"Me, a fish? A Tokay plant?" Cladan asked out loud, drying his hair with a towel.

"What slinking, dewlapped, piccalilli boil of a mool shuttles the dusty ears of cacao to circle home?" he said into the face of her pop, who only looked back stunned at him; less for what was said, but more for the way it was said to him.

"The nepaline bears that nestle in the lucent snow?" Cladan asked the others.

He cupped his mouth as he drunkenly yelled up to the poplar trees surrounding the manicured yard. *"You tuft clump of hell-flakes hankering by the ivy!"*

Fintonia sniggered as he suddenly pointed to the sky the other way.

"Look! Cupid's bucket of piss is a blistering storm!"

With everyone looking up, he bent towards a few old seated matriarchs, then reeled back like he'd just got wind of a seal. *"Cop the moneyed banks of the Royal mint!"*

And he left, staggering off drunk down the driveway, saluting a statue in the garden on his way out...

Days later, Fintonia rang him, and asked if he was coming in to work.

He said no. He'd had it with it all. His elbows burned from all the scrubbing.

She could tell he was drinking.

She told him she'd been warned not to see him anymore. He was *"emotionally dangerous"* her family had said.

"Families say the worst things," he slurred to her. *"Mercenaries, the lot of them. After a while, as the years pass, when the talk wears thin, and the same old pap revolves within the pack, everyone just telegraphs their moves, like a bunch of staged musketeers crashing about in the mud. But when their swords snap in halves, and everyone's stuck without a prompt, they just stare back at each other, dumb for cues, saying their old lines again. Then someone falters, by saying something else for once, and in the air is the off scent of blood, and like vampires your relatives just dive in and finish you off."*

29
TO TOSS A COIN
CAN HIDE THE SUN

Fintonia stood on the veranda in her wedding veil and underwear, sipping at a flute of bubbly as she watched the ocean in the distance still rising above the riverbanks, swamping the tulip farm in the valley below. Beyond the palm trees dotting the lagoons, a swarm of army choppers slowly shifted across the sky like a wall of pelicans.

Cladan stepped out of the cabin in his underwear, and with her knee-high wedding boots on, gnawing on a drumstick. She smirked on spotting him in her get-up again as he put a small pair of binoculars to his eyes.

"They're saving Phi Phi Island first," he slurred.

Then he ravished his wife right there on the veranda again, as she laughed her head off like she had for days. No one was around for miles. It was a prize honeymoon spot ...

At dusk, sitting on the steps of the cabin, by their moored wooden junk — just in case — Fintonia dangled her toes in the river as Cladan gently plucked a splinter from her knee with tweezers. Then more choppers crossed the reddened sky, heading back the other way.

"I hope they never come for us," she cooed, as she downed another glass.

"If the volcano doesn't pop, we're fine," Cladan softly said as he concentrated.

"I hope they all crash," she snapped back.

Cladan gently kissed her knee for medicinal purposes as she emptied the bottle of bubbly into their glasses. Then there was nothing but silence for a while as they stared out towards the fading horizon.

"It's so quiet," Fintonia sighed. *"I think all the pygmy elephants drowned."*

"Probably washed into the mud springs," Cladan said, tipping his glass back. *"They'd all be cooked by now."*

"You wanna carve?" she said drolly, gulping at her drink.

"Everything should be pre-cooked anyway," Cladan slurred, suddenly hiccupping.

Fintonia drunkenly sniggered through her nose in little broken hisses as she stared ahead at the failing sky.

Cladan downed the rest of his drink.

"If you're peckish," he continued, *"you just walk up to something and take your best chomp. This railing."*

"Everything," Fintonia grandly declared, sweeping the whole disaster unfolding in front of them with her glass, *"must be eaten!"*

And they devoured each other again like cannibals for the millionth time since their wedding — laughing crazy, biting hot, wet, and greedy for each other. Whilst in the distance, a lone gibbon faintly wailed in the flood drowning the valley below . . .

Entwined naked in a hammock between two palms as advertised, Fintonia rested her head on Cladan's chest in the moonlight, and they both just stared up at the stars. Though they soon slipped back into their old post-coital American pillow-talk routine, like they often did for a laugh before falling asleep in each other's arms when they were spent and happy.

"Hoagy?" she suddenly whined out loud, like she was straight off the Mississippi delta.

Cladan's chest faintly bounced her head up and down as he silently chuckled to himself for a second: it was just the way she said it, after such a long and golden silence between them. And even though he couldn't see her face, he knew she was happy too: the edges of her giant smile subtly tugged at the skin of his stomach a little.

"I don't want no else round, but choo," she said, sounding tired and a little mean. *"I despise people, like my mammy said. I don't wanna see no more agin. Period."*

"Just you and me, my little prairie fire?" Cladan mumbled in a southern twang.

She sniggered.

"And no one else," she suddenly seethed. *"That's dang for sure."*

When morning came, Fintonia woke alone, looking towards the open window and the hum of all the choppers flying by in the distance again. She could see Cladan standing naked on a ridge in just his sandals, with a drink in one hand, and aiming a bamboo broom up at the choppers with the other, pretending to fire off a few rounds, complete with sound effects as they passed by.

"And d-o-o-o-n't y-o-u for-git it!" he hollered out after them, doing his worst Quick Draw McGraw.

And then he heard his wife playfully cooing out loud in bed to him, and he turned to see her giggling in fits as she leaned on the window sill with her breasts exposed, and he ran back down the hill and into the cabin again, all messed up and dirty, with mud smeared all over him, laughing wild like the last man on earth.

"Home at last, Dorothy! Home at last!"

And she burst out laughing, and they made love again and again, like it really was the end of the world and only left to them to replenish it, if they wanted to.

30
CHRISTENDOM
AT THIRD HAND

In a tropical Queensland town, full of de-skilled fleas and barfly bars, Cladan breathed out a bloated sigh as he read the killer's last words splashed across the front page of the local rag:

"IF THERE IS A LIE,
THAT THING IS A
COVENANT OF LOVE."

Since blocking the only road out of town, the few local cops left over went off on a sly manhunt in disguise and snuck in amongst all the town's bums, thinking the killer might have dressed down and tried to blend in for a while before a subtle getaway: but the bums always said nothing to those in chase of anyone. A week earlier, someone in the middle of the night had stabbed the dozing guard at the town's only tollbooth a dozen times across the gullet, and in the perforated shape of the cross.

"ONE SLIT PER APOSTLE" was the cheap headline.

The speed camera caught nothing; but the booth's intercom recorded the sound of a man's laughter in the background, *"like a cackling dolphin,"* and possibly the faint footsteps of an unannounced accomplice.

Soon, a few big-badged sleuths from the big smoke in Brisbane turned up and got all forensic in their zipper suits everywhere, blasting the tape raw to zero in on the key. Then they started hanging out at the local laughing store just to see if they could ever nab him by sound. They were soon hurting everyone else in retaliation though. It was more a show of power; a display of bravado. All their city kudos on the loose. But it all went haywire in the end. They'd find all sorts of combos and mark them down for a time.

TABLE #02: A he who HAWS, with a she who HA'S.

TABLE #09: A she who ROARS, with a he who AH'S.

Then they got all cocky about it, and started taking in all those off the street, and tickling them to death with a duster to match the sound. It was a shantytown at heart. Anyone only had to ever bark at someone wrong and everything else rolled on further like a tipped row of dominoes to the other end till someone was finally clean hooked through the gums and bottled for all to ogle.

But a wound of the cross?

And then all of a sudden, a hung priest in the town's only chapel, leaving only a headline for a note? It all soon added up to everyone, figuring the faint steps of the accomplice on the tape was in fact his fat pet Alsatian, Gavolga, who he'd strung up right alongside himself in the confessional booth opposite.

An old local hero, Blibby Ravoochy, who ran an emu farm for tourists on the edge of town, had become friends with Fintonia and Cladan as they both hunkered down for a three month stint there as fruit pickers to muster up enough cash for a deposit on a house back down in Melbourne. Blibby had intermittently served time behind bars in town over the last five years for publicly declaring his soul.

"Or whatever this thing is," as he always said, slapping a hand at his guts.

His chief offence? Once a year, on the anniversary of the town's council election, he'd ceremoniously walk up to the corrupt town mayor lunching in a nearby café, and tip a bucket of fresh doo from his farm all over his meal, and simply say straight-faced to him, something like, *"A man from Venus toils worse,"* and then he'd just head off back home to promptly feed his giant birds.

He'd kept this feud going over a simple by-law for five years running, claiming it was the *"Irrepealable statement of my community conscience,"* from which all the other locals had long shied away from ever openly expressing, but secretly endorsed in privacy among themselves. Blibby thought it was the best form of revenge. He had a set formula for modern acts of revolt to help change the sluggish world. Novelty + notoriety = attention.

"No matter what churlish action is ever bestowed," he'd drunkenly spiel, *"it always lodges itself deep in the clocked psyche of the baaing constituency."*

He'd planned to continue doing it right down to the last days of the mayor's final term in office, and he was always letting loose some senseless astronomical riddle as a clincher at the end of every spill, like *"Here's a sip from Jupe."*

"Just to confuse the Crown of all intent," he'd whisper, tapping at his temple. *"This town's got no rubber palace,"* he'd say, gently elbow-jabbing any secret admirer who'd briefly sidle up to honour him on his way about town, wishing him luck, and calling him a genius.

Blibby was long the darling rebel of all the town's underdogs, but soon the years had moved on, and they were all slowly dying off as well, and Blibby was running out of time too, and he knew it. A month or two locked up in the city pound each year had ground his business down into the dust, defeating the fight for the flexible trading hours he'd always wanted in the first place. And most of his birds were dying because of the boycott of grain slyly imposed on him by the surrounding municipalities long chummy with the mayor and his family. Some old-time local farmers were pushing for him to get life the next time around, simply for tipping crud on a two-bit official of a nowhere town on the edge of the beyond. No one would even dare sell him a chip bucket in the end, just to make sure he couldn't keep it all going as usual for another year.

Fintonia and Cladan had been trying to calm Blibby down, because he was getting inconsolably drunk all the time, feeling like everything was pointless in the end. His wife was dead. His grown children were dead. And all his birds were dying.

He kept on talking of the ships sailing out from the desert to save him at last, instead of just looking right behind him, where they were all moored, just waiting to take him away wherever he wanted. Everyone had seen the odd one here or there slowly succumb to the sandstorms' legendary madness.

But Fintonia and Cladan were only passing through, and didn't really know much about it all — the town's history, and all its ways — and initially took Blibby for a man of reckless wisdom, by all the word of mouth he seemed to be getting. But they soon saw it for what it was — the end of whim. The same old tale they'd both ever seen unfold everywhere themselves.

Blibby would just sit drunk in the shadows of his ragged tent, in the empty corral, mumbling and raving.

"Everyone's told," he rambled, rocking back and forth. *"Everyone's sold. Everyone folds."*

Cladan would try to ease him up, but Blibby never did again shift from his new gaze, forever stuck there on his haunches, rocking on his spine, dreaming, raving, amazed at the way everything had suddenly changed, mulling over the crippling effect of the sanctions on his dream and livelihood, with all the tourists far away.

Cladan suggested to him, somewhat desperate to help, that, in a way, he might be free.

"Free?" Blibby slurred. *"That's the zip of death. The waving world. Freedom? It's all a lie, a covenant of love. Like the man said. Free's just a stink passing by. Nothing stays. It turns with the wind, and goes on, burning all. Some silly odour it is, skipping loose across the nose. Probably slogging it out on some God-green lawn a world away now, with a whole clan happy to be hoodwinked at last."*

Cladan rubbed at his eyes, blinking.

"Forget about it, you two. Everyone cups in low now. You'll see. The ineptitude of a passing throng, bound right round the ball."

Cladan stared ahead in a drunken daze to the desert's horizon wavering in the distance as Fintonia stared the other way to the line across the sea, before dropping her head onto her bag and napping out from all the beer.

"Hey. Don't give those scared looks for me," Blibby said with a smile to Cladan. *"Being scared's the sillier tune, you dippy pig."*

Cladan smiled back at him again, but a little forcefully, cranking it up again on each side of his sun‑swollen face, but it seemed much more heavier this final time they'd ever share a drink together.

"That's it," squealed Blibby with a lopsided smirk, *"Pig it, piggy. Oink it."*

Cladan briefly chuckled back — more to cheer him up — then accidentally snorted.

And Blibby fell back, laughing his head off, laying about the rotting carcasses of his giant birds, all of them smothered with blowflies dropping maggots under their massive wings like bombs.

32

ALONG THE COOL
SEQUESTERED VALE

At dawn, a pair of flirting wattlebirds slowly dueled their Tarzanic cries across a bend in the Yarra — each song bouncing from bank to bank beneath the mist — but Cladan didn't hear a thing. Only his muddied boots could be seen poking out of the weeds as he lay snoring in a corner of the park. Then he rolled over onto his stomach, and his hands curled back over his shoulders to keep himself warm. A dark wet patch was on his back from drunkenly rolling over in the dew, and his fingers were white from the cold, just like it used to happen to his ma. Soon, a magpie added an eerie tune, delicately warbling to one side.

Not far from Cladan, lying asleep in leaves and nettles, was his wife, facing the other way in the fetal position: a vomit patch freshly scorched into the kept lawn just broaching her toes.

Over by the river, a few ducks softly quacked amongst the cries, fresh out from their shacks the bushes. The massive sky, crisp and clear, and faintly lime. Then a dozen cars somewhere sat on their horns, scaring the littler birds, who all gathered in the arms of a giant ghost gum ready to suck in the morning smog.

Cladan spluttered, and suddenly shook awake with a shudder rolling up his spine like a xylophone. He could barely lift his head, and — taking on the weight of his hangover — gently wiped his whiskered face into the frosty grass to clear his eyes and stretch his stiff mouth. Then he propped himself up on an elbow and looked around, trying to work out where the hell they were. He thought he could hear a freeway nearby, but couldn't work out where.

Slung across the trunk of a nearby tree was an old rusty bike with question mark handlebars, the type he'd always hated.

One from the do? he wondered, looking at it with a frown, sure he'd never seen it before, trying to remember who could have ever pedaled it. Fintonia? Himself? Who could have ever dinked who about in their colossal stupor the night before? Not much seemed to be obvious at such an early hour.

Then she stirred awake — but she wasn't who he thought she was. This woman was quicker. She sat up straight, looking off, and got to her feet with a stagger, then buttoned her jeans and tiptoed across the park in her bare feet, without looking back at him. Cladan watched her as she stopped in the middle of a sunny footy oval in the distance and picked up a couple of things, then she wiped them on the grass and put them on her feet and walked on, appearing suddenly ganglier.

Cladan clutched at the bike, but found it locked to the trunk with a chain. So he slowly stumbled the last mile home against the Monday morning racket ...

Climbing the stairs to the veranda of his little fibro home, Cladan spat in the garden patch, landing a gob right inside the last withered marigold, and shoved open the wobbly front door — the same door he'd twice had to pry open with a screwdriver to get in because his wife couldn't wake up.

But Fintonia was often missing at times, or late as well. Her whereabouts forgotten.

Her adventures unknown. Her face like his — craggy and swollen from all the drink.

Cladan gazed at the usual trailing clumps of muck smeared across the carpet, leading up the hallway to the bathroom door. One look at each other and they'd either laugh out of remorse, or motion one another to the bed, or the shower, sometimes scrubbing each other down in the silence, comparing dirt, like chimps with fleas.

They weren't too familiar when they spoke anymore. That was an unwritten law.

Comfortable? Not by the longest shot — but they were trying to own the dump. It was the cheapest suburb in town. Rusted shells of old cars lay in all the paddocks around. The yellow grasses high as reeds by the neighbour's leaning grey fences. It wasn't much of a suburb, yet everyone seemed to be flocking there.

33
THE SONGS OF
CONFERENCE HALLS

It was Friday night and Cladan was back at work, rubbing the Hoover hard into the office carpet, trying to suck up the dead moths under the blinds, when a Japanese woman in a white wet suit scrambled into the office and hid behind the door, sniggering in her snorkel. He looked up at her as he kept on vacuuming, but with a pressed finger to her mask she sneakily slipped out from her hiding spot and rushed back down the corridor. No one else was around. It was an hour past lock-up.

"Are you there, Pip?" a man garbled from an intercom on a desk. *"You there?"*

Out of Cladan's eyeline the elevator opened up and a silver-haired Superman leaned out with a brandy in hand and whistled down the corridor. The woman soon rushed back, and stepped inside with him, laughing her head off, then the elevator went down two floors, and all the lights suddenly went out — the Hoover winding down like the turbine of a jet.

Cladan felt his way to the elevator, and punched at the buttons, but nothing happened. Clutching at a rail in the dark, he headed down the emergency stairway for two flights, then tripped over a couple rutting on the landing, and opened the emergency-door, only to find himself smack-dab in the middle of a fancy dress office party swamping the entire level.

Giant roosters were strutting about, as feral knights in Mad Max armour started swinging foam lances at everybody in sight. Cackling insects were floating by with drinks in every claw, and spiders at the stalls gorged down party pies by the dozen like it was a contest. Zydeco music blared out from one corner, and jelly wrestling jostled in another.

Over near the emergency exit, old schoolgirls with long grey plats were skipping around balding altar boys playing the drums. Everyone was decked out in homemade costumes, drinking cocktails, and throwing back shots and popping pills all over the place.

Cladan just stood there with his mouth open like a kid at the circus.

Everyone was dancing, and spilling drinks, and smearing meatballs and cake into the carpet — a mess he knew he'd be stuck with mopping up on his next shift. The idea of quitting quickly crossed his mind, then the shy receptionist from downstairs sailed past him — naked in a paper mache bathtub — as she drunkenly cooeed to a Batman bouncing by on a pogo-stick with his tongue hanging out.

"S'always the quiet ones," Cladan said, grinning to an alien as he walked through the pack with his brushes still clipped to his belt, his Windex back-pocketed, a dirty chamois hanging through the straps of his overalls. He soon felt like he was just playing a role as well, instead of doing his job, and he snatched a flaming goblet from a passing tray, and sat on a desk and gulped it down, watching on, though keeping an eye out for his boss, just in case.

In the middle of the office, a triple tiered fountain spewed red punch high into the air. Crustaceans were nattering, and clattering, dipping conches in and out.

High above everyone, a cop was swinging on a trapeze, and a gorilla was throwing chocolate crackles at his back, giggling under his mask as each one exploded like a cluster bomb over everyone falling about drunk on the dance floor below.

To one side, a bald woman with cobwebs tattooed on each side of her nose scooped a hand up and down an aquarium, trying to catch an axolotl swimming around terrified.

And all around the tall windows, balloons were slowly popping off from the lit candles below, giving the party the constant atmosphere of champagne.

Cladan opened a door in a corner of the office and moonlight shimmered into the room like a mirror, bouncing off all the inebriated eyes and glasses. Outside on the landing were more sloshed Caesars bubbling up. Waiters in G-strings squeezed through the crowd as drunken nuns reached out for quick feels on their way back inside. Everyone was smoking joints, and burbling bongs, and snorting junk off the long chromed rail bordering the balcony.

There were women wrapped in sheets, and men coiled in reams of alfoil, with their genitals hanging out, all bowed up in ribbons and holly. Marilyns were rife, as were Elvi and Acid Queens. And hanging over a rail, a grenadier vomited blue, 17 floors straight down.

Glasses were endlessly smashing inside, with the music stamping through the wall, and the door was swinging open and shut like the whole building was breathing.

Nearby, King Neptune gorged on butterflies on toast as he watched a mummy whittle a stuffed tortoise into an ashtray for the Holy Ghost. And then a monk turned on a hose, spraying everyone, but no one flinched from the cold — everyone stuck their feet out to be blessed, laughing out of their nostrils in white clouds of dust, like newly hatched galaxies just released from the polyps of a whole new wheeling void.

A subtle fog slowly settled across the roofs of the higher skyscrapers, as the moon rolled behind a cloud like an old record being slipped back into its battered sleeve.

Cladan was sitting by a hydrant, guzzling on a bottle of beer, as he paper-rock-scissored for the hundredth time with a pissed sheik covered in blood — but he soon went back inside, looking for the bog. Nurses were tagging hearts on the walls with satchels of sauce. Scotsmen were playing naughts and crosses with all the dips. Beards primped into flowers. Eyebrows swirled into dots. A lone cricketer softly droned on a bassoon whilst watching a gangster lipsticking a judge; as a few vicars played croquet down a corridor, using someone's prosthetic leg as their only mallet.

Cladan polished off the bottle and crawled tightly along a wall.

On the tiled floor in the Men's lay scattered leaves and cracked cockleshells. He opened a cubicle, only to find his boss sitting smashed on the bowl, in the guise of a matador, trying to scale a barracuda with his mobile phone. But Cladan averted his eyes and headed to the urinal instead, and finally let all the liquor flow free. On the wall, fresh messages to browse as he swayed...

> "Marion Crane was fucked
> up the arse 709 times
> as advertised"

All those twisted things he'd long had to scrub off the amenity walls of every floor. Then a bearded woman ran in drunk, and hugged him tightly around his waist as he peed, crooning like a torch-singer in his ear...

> *"Let me feel your burdens dwindle,*
> *Till they only fill a thimble,*
> *A specious space,*
> *Like a sock hole,*
> *Long lost and unloved;*
> *Coz I am*
> *Your sock of love. "*

Eventually he finished, in tight inhibited squirts and dribbles, and she darted back out the door, loudly yodeling.

Cladan looked in the mirror as he washed his hands and face, and let loose a long echoing beer burp. Then he pulled a mad face at himself, and yowled for the hell of it, and raced back out into the screaming racket again. It was like a fuse was lit inside himself and he couldn't get to oblivion fast enough. He sculled down as much punch as he could muster and danced with a green girl dressed only in gumboots. He subtly watched a witch to one side sucking on the horn of a rhino, as nearby, a black angel licked clean the lint from a bodybuilder's navel, who seemed to be more nurtured by the bristles of her burnt fluffy wings.

In the corner, the grim reaper played paddy whack with a sphinx, as a kneeling Greek girl in mourning, with moles all over her face, stood perfectly still whilst a jockey joined all her dots with a texta to draw a horse.

Then an Arafat started shooting out the flames of all the candles with a slingshot, and all the vendors started shooting ping-pong balls across the crowd from both sides, as paralytic sailors flicked the lights off and on to the hammering music, till it all ended up looking like the end of the world.

But Cladan had enough, and soon staggered off to catch a train; and the stark realisation of how he'd suddenly lost his youth sourly occupied his mind all the way home.

He found Fintonia watching TV in the corner of the lounge, breastfeeding their son, Fort, whilst knitting his New Year footy-beanie. She looked at him with tears in her eyes as he approached her. Then he leaned down, and delicately held her face in his hands, and kissed her passionately, their tongues dueling for the first time in centuries, as a contestant on a game show slammed her buzzer down and shrieked *"Iodine!"* at the top of her lungs.

35
THE NEW SOUP

Fintonia sloshed the teaspoon around till the milk turned brown, and tinked it on the edge of the glass a couple of times like she was playing a triangle in a band, then stepped back into the lounge and handed it over to Cladan — his eyes still glued to the cricket on TV.

"Tah," he said, without looking up at her.

She went straight back to the ironing board as Cladan put the tall glass straight to his lips, and a large lily pad of Milo on top still swirled in a whirlpool so fast, that when he first sipped at it, it tugged on his top lip a bit, dragging him in, and as he greedily swilled it all down in one hit, he felt it spinning weirdly evil around his teeth: all of it dropping down his throat in broken clumps, leaving his mouth webbed thick with strings of mucous.

He suddenly leapt up from his spine, with his mouth hanging wide, and dived past Fintonia to the kitchen sink, and induced a spell of vomiting all over the dishes, gasping for water from the tap.

"Wrong pipe?" she asked out loud as she laid out her frilly white skirt.

Cladan guzzled and gargled, then opened the fridge and pulled out the carton of milk and shook it about — only to hear it rattling like a maraca as he feared. He read the use-by date on the spout, then glared back at his wife through the glass cabinet separating the kitchenette from the lounge, his mouth hung open like a gully trap.

"What are you doing to me?" he gibbered.

"Hey?"

"The use-by date's last month. There's lumps in it the size of Saturn!"

"Oh. Sorry."

"Sorry doesn't feed the buffalo porridge," he snapped, as he leant back into the fridge. *"Ok, the best's for Fort, but I'd rather have nothing than off milk, alright? Don't save the shit milk for us. Throw the shit milk out."*

He pulled a few more cartons out.

"Can't you toss all these?"

Then a silence fell between them — one of the recurring many — as Cladan slumped back onto the couch and watched TV again, opening his last can of beer. Fintonia resumed her ironing, and folded all their ragged clothes in the quiet as the commentators endlessly blathered. But Cladan was still too steamed, and during an ad break just had to pursue it further. There was nothing else to do.

"Food poisoning with chicken, I'm fine with," he said sourly. *"And poultry's the worst. But not dairy products. It clings to the linings of your gut so the acid can't work, then you get indigestion, then constipation, then you die."*

"Okay!" she snapped back, holding out the iron, hissing steam back at him.

Cladan flicked the channel: a mud-caked goalie jumped out from a net and missed a soccer ball. Flicked: worm pills. Flicked: a burning church. Flicked: back to the midday news about the story on found brains.

Then their baby cried out loud.

"Where's the dummy?" Fintonia asked.

"I don't know," Cladan mumbled. *"Can't you feed him."*

"I've nothing left," she softly said.

Cladan suddenly raced out of the flat and scrambled down the rickety stairs to the street, almost screaming. Then the postie peddled towards him, filling up letterboxes.

"Any for flat 19?" he barked out loud in the dead suburban silence.

The postie looked up from under her hat like a country 'n' western star as she pulled up and flipped through the mail in her crate. Cladan started rolling a smoke, and then she plucked out a manila envelope and handed it over. But he playfully opened up his mouth as he rolled, and she reluctantly put it between his teeth and peddled away, sneering at how pleased with himself he seemed. Income tax slip — $49 owed. He'd paid a fortune in tax over the last year for peanuts, and they were still living on beetroot and mashed potato sandwiches.

He walked on to the shops, thinking *What A Wonderful World* as a white cat tiptoed across a fence top above his head.

"You know what gets me?" Cladan whined to the old bored shopkeeper seated at his till. *"Not that we can't eat, or that the baby screams night and day, or my toes are hanging out of my boots like sardines, but just everything, you know? The way everything's just an outright lie. The things we're told. The things we tell. On and on, the same every day.*

The continual monotony of all the same old stupid lies."

The shopkeeper slowly nodded in agreement like a sympathetic barman fixing him a drink.

"Wouldn't mind heading up north somewhere," Cladan wondered aloud. *"Tucked away from everything. On the edge of nowhere. Open to the elements. Blue skies all day. Sand in your ears. The ocean all around. You know, out of the rat race altogether. Completely free."*

The barman sighed, party to the dream.

"Then there's the tourists, and all that game," Cladan said, suddenly sour again, picking up the plastic bag from the counter. *"The same old thing in another dress. No difference. Same rats. Same race."*

Cladan fished out the coins, counting them up, but he was a little short, and he promised to make up the difference the next time he was in as usual.

On the way home he sipped a little at the milk, trying to rinse out the taste of all those sour blobs he'd downed earlier that the beer couldn't budge, and spat white everywhere in glowing splashes all the way up the street towards home ...

36

A KISS CRACKS LIKE
A THUNDERCLAP

After work Cladan downed a few drinks at a nearby bar during Happy Hour where he was served by a singing dwarf called Zee, who was sitting on the shoulders of another dwarf (her husband, Beau) who passed up the glasses and harmonised the songs. But when they started in on *The Lion Sleeps Tonight*, Cladan tipped himself out of his stool and drunkenly lumbered off towards Flinders Street Station to get the train home.

He despised that song, but it kept on spinning around in his head. On the way, he briefly surrendered to daydreaming about dwarves to drown it out, and about living his life as one...

Cladan could see himself tipped back in a dentist's chair, stretching his tiny mouth wide as a burping orthodontist — with seeping cold sores, bloodshot eyes, and a pyre whiskey breath — nearly emptied his entire tray of tools down his throat. With his little jaws locked open, and his eyes frying hard under the light, the orthodontist screamed down "Wider!" at him, then jabbed a needle right through his tongue, just missing his gums, and the sting ricocheted all over his baby face like he'd just been electrocuted. Cladan blindly lashed out, and poked this butcher in the eyes, then bashed his jaw about like a parking meter, knocking him to the floor. Then he slid out of the chair and jumped up and down on his chest, then quickly rinsed, and left, with the bib still around his neck — the nurses ringing the police.

"Calling all cars. APB on local hood, Cladan Kareeda, for assaulting a tooth quack. Caucasian midget. Receding red hair. Four bottom teeth. Very stroppy. Approach with caution. Locale is... "

In the rocking carriage, bored commuters stared into the dead spots between themselves as a mime artist pretended to read a newspaper to one side and started to nod off. Then he jolted awake again, checking his tie, his shoelaces, his fly, licking back his hair like a mane, and inevitably realised he was stuck behind an invisible wall. Sitting opposite: Cladan, all fired up, with a dead tongue stuck in his throat. He was in no mood for muck. He hated mime more than life itself, and loathed artists of every calibre. When the train pulled into Murrumbeena station, he punched him hard in the eggs, and disembarked, then clambered through Parker Park, throwing pinecones at all the hip-swivellers racing around everywhere, mad as geese. Down dead suburban streets, he ripped the lids off letterboxes and tore up the local papers. He snapped an aerial off a car and thrashed a row of rose bushes down to the bones. But, once home, he soon calmed himself down, watching his favourite prison serial on TV as he delicately sipped at a mushroom cup-a-soup out of the corner of his mouth. "Alright, Cladan!" a man suddenly blared from a megaphone outside. "Come on out, with all 10 snags locked across the melon ball, or you're one dead, blood-nutted troll!" His tiny hands curled into tight baby fists on hearing all the laughter erupt outside. There was no time for plans. Then the phone rang. He grabbed it fast, peering through the blinds, just above the sill, to see three police cars with flashing lights, and a squad of cops kneeling behind doors, cocking shotguns. "Son?" blubbered Cladan's father on the other end of the line. "This is the other Cladan. I'm sorry." Cladan scoffed out loud and hung up, cocking the derringer in his little trench coat. Then he pounded it against the window, but it wouldn't smash, so he stood on a stool to do it properly. The BOOM BOOM BOOM of shotguns pumping into his silhouetted frame echoed down the street for blocks as he fell tangled up in the venetian blinds. Days later, all the local wharfies and union reps attended his funeral in the rain. He was wheeled through the empty streets on the back of his mentor's infamous Billy cart, and buried in a tea chest in Dwarf Lot, the gangster wing of Small Hood Pines ...

Nearing the station, Cladan snapped out of his dream as he spotted some sort of a commotion going on over in Banana Alley. Blinding light was streaming out into the street like there was a laser show. Then he realised a movie was being made, so he wandered over for a browse like everyone else.

Extras dressed as orderlies and nurses were standing around smoking near a few hospital dumpsters, and watching a dozen skimpy vampires do a tambourine dance in a trance. Then an explosion ripped through the throng, spilling guts and limbs everywhere, as robotic bats wheeled down on wires and began to suck at all the bloodied stumps.

During preparations for another take, a young actress in a strange garb walked back down Banana Alley the other way to start again. Some of the crew was teasing her about her character being called Vohulima Banjax, and how she was supposed to be a pranayama yoga sect queen, and she was jokingly whistling the theme song of Beany and Cecil the Sea-Sick Sea Serpent all the way past them as if blocking it all out. Then she stopped in her tracks for a chat with a gaffer, talking about some odd jobs she'd had over the years, laughing about how one night she brazenly moonlighted as a lassoist when she ran out of hot dogs.

Cladan was standing close by in the crowd, looking at her in her zany costume. But something twigged about her profile, and her white hair. Then she turned, and he saw her face in full, and realised she was the very first love of his life — old Amber Greely, from all those years ago at Our Immanuel of the Most Precious Blood. And he immediately felt guilty about never saying goodbye to her that day, when he was wrenched from the only school he ever loved and thrown into another life. It seemed a hasty step to go over and talk to her, but he was all fired up on Dutch courage and couldn't let it go.

"*Am?*" he said out loud to her, a little unsure he was doing the right thing.

Amber turned to him, and in the space of just four seconds, recognised him as quickly as he'd recognised her, then turned away.

He didn't know what to do. Was she still mad at him after all this time?

Then a tall man, around Cladan's age, with a briefcase in hand, suddenly approached her, and they began to chat to one side for a while like they were friends. Which was a double whammy for Cladan. The man was an old local acquaintance from Cladan's neighbourhood when he was a teen, who he'd roughly known, but hadn't seen about in years: Buch Phuk, of the Gung-Gung-Phuks. Moles flecked all over his face. And he was still the brain.

Buch was now a well-to-do maths lecturer, as expected, and he was telling Amber about how he'd always been a numbers man at heart who loved to watch ballerinas up on their big toes. Though it was the eight littler ones aloof, always hanging aloft by the pivoting stubs, that were the inspiration for his work, and the foundation of his PhD on electro-gravitism, which a few think tanks overseas were eager to nibble at.

Buch said he'd studied the ballet extensively over the years as a result of his research, and he talked to her openly about all the nightmares he'd had about the dance at large; hearing in his sleep the first tortured pirouette screams of Reieve, Marie Taglioiv, and the Grand Jete of Svetlana Benosova. Buch said he'd watched these goddesses as tiny ghosts in his laboratory twirling gracefully on the tips of all the foam cones across his bench tops when the sunlight was just right.

Then, leaning in closer to Buch, Amber very delicately imparted the warmest, gentlest smile to him, her eyes gleaming.

All he could see, Buch shyly continued, were these haunting thoughts of logarithms and cosines in everything around him, and how everything he saw seemed but a constant regret in joy — like a hoary snail encompassing its sleeve for the want of at least a lesser burden.

Cladan suddenly bounded up to them, in a desperate drunken attempt to sabotage anything developing further between them, and he slurred to Amber that, *"Buch is an egghead, and he knows it."*

Buch didn't recognise him at first, and neither of them said anything back to him.

But Cladan continued, and he told Amber that the ultimate skill Buch had long sought to develop as a teen was to be able to say exactly what someone else was saying, at exactly the same time, with every person he met. He told her that Buch once said to him that he knew if this was ever possible to achieve, he would *"one day make it big in showbiz, and become the world's most famous arithmetical star, and somehow find true happiness in the process."*

Cladan thought this childish notion might put her off, hoping it might illustrate perfectly how Buch was completely wrong for her, how he was essentially addled, and shallow at heart, and how then she might see himself as a more earthy man in practical matters of the world and bid for him instead. But then, Buch and Amber suddenly turned and looked at each other and smiled, and said, *"I love you,"* at exactly the same time, then tenderly kissed.

Floored, Cladan slowly turned away in shock without a word, and wavered back up the alley through the crowd, and staggered off in tears towards the station again, feeling like he'd just seen God at work, and was convinced his days were numbered, sure that he'd die young in the end, and that it would not be long before he would duly greet death...

37

THE DAYS SCATTER LIKE MICE FEELING SEEN

The relentless squalls had become unbearable for the last few months; the way they screamed at night. Cladan soon gave up on ever trying to fire up the leaky cooking lamp again, so he'd started eating vegies straight from the can instead, and he'd just listen to the roars of the winds and the waves. His face was scabbed and he had a scraggly beard and a mop of knotted hair. But, in the end he'd had enough of it all — the cold, the dark, the sea ghosts, the stars — so he packed up his tent and left the sands.

He didn't know what day it was, or exactly what month. An eternity had gone by on the dunes since his escape from his wife. He'd watched the cycles of nature unfurl for so long, all of it building and dissolving, taking in the way each season would subtly alter the hidden corner of every hollow, and all he could ever think of all the while to compensate were her smouldering eyes.

Dreaming like a madman by the shore for so long, Cladan had seen the faces of his oldest friends gurgling in the silver wash of every breaker — ones of betrayal mostly — pondering over the way so few alien others had ever slipped into their broken spaces. Each wave had flooded his eyes with memories of all those old times he'd once freely surrendered to and cherished, and time after time he'd always wade in up to his waist to embrace them all — and as each one disintegrated in crashes upon him, he wondered how one day the sea would be sold as just another property, and how all of his old friends would long be traded ...

He could see the slick city landmark ahead, stuck bombastically in the sky like the barb of a vegetable, with the cold moon skewered at the base of it, *"Where All Grief Lies Vanquished At Last,"* arrogantly on show for everyone.

Cladan imagined a white meridian line of the globe inching across the night sky, leading him back to her door like the star of antiquity. The same way as when, only the year before, he'd lost all his senses and wandered off alone — guided by a singular cloud — till he reached the coast, and settled there, with the idea of refuting any need to belong to anyone again. He long dreamed of remaining there till he was just a wasted fossil on the shore, a prop for all the lovers ambling by to pick up and whistle tunes with.

In the laneways of his hometown, Cladan caught sight of the first two neighbours in his street he'd ever known, stumbling out of the local tavern — still both screaming high-pitched murderous cries at one another. But they didn't recognise him — the way he looked like a bum — and as he walked on, stumbling around the streets at midnight, he could soon feel all the old wheels in his mind beginning to whirr free again; all the spokes flicking off the recent months like mud as they turned; their hubs crying out all the old cries again, echoing off the factory walls, dissipating amongst the fields.

It was home time in hometown, and Cladan was hauling in all sorts of memories. His eyes welling up as he looked around at everything so familiar to him. And it wasn't because of a wind carrying a million sands in a storm this time, or the sun scorching off the shore and distilling all his visions. There was no blame on seasons anymore. All that had lifted as if it'd never been. It suddenly felt a crime to even dare redress that whole Hell again — how he'd hid away from her, and then from everyone. And as the ice from the splint long binding him slowly melted back into his blood and bones again, he recanted to himself once more as he walked on just as determined as he used to be.

He rapped the knocker of his old haunt, where she'd once long rapped for him at night the year before. Where, in the corner of the veranda, whacked out of her mind, she'd huddle in tears, waiting for him to come home, or to come out to her — sometimes squatted on the doormat to keep warm, leaving distinct marks of sweat, once of menses, twice of weight, and all the while crying out his last words to her like a caterwaul. But on that stoop he now revered, all he could see were the remains of rats in the shadows, frozen in winter's embrace.

The hour was late, and the dew was already down, spread thinly like the fire he'd drunkenly set the year before; but the fibro walls were still sturdy and only a skerrick of the old ash still showed about the edges of the sill. And he immediately hated himself for that. And then he hated what she did all over again. And he could suddenly feel all the old storms brewing in his mind again — like once a week in the olden days when all the parties fell apart. But just before he felt like pounding on the splintered door, it suddenly opened up to him, and her new sugar daddy was standing there, wearing sunglasses and a frown. He was small, but creaking weights up and down with a tattooed arm.

Cladan could hear Fintonia laughing at the TV from the far room down the hall. And he could see her skimpy costumes hanging to the side on a line of hooks. But this pimp was blind, and seemed no immediate threat to him. Cladan then tried to talk in reasonable terms with him, putting his hands down — seeing that the man couldn't see — but it was the first time he'd spoken to anyone all year, and as he began to talk, he suddenly rambled out of breath like his life was just a spool that was all along unraveling itself. He felt like a madman on just hearing himself speak. It was a sudden knowledge, and distaste to him, after enduring such a long and laborious incubation to steady himself and return replenished to her.

Then a silhouette of another man appeared at the tall wire gate behind him.

Cladan turned around and felt a sudden surge of fear dance across his skin. Then he murmured a heartfelt plea to just see his wife and son once again, as both men in unison counted out loud for him to promptly leave the property.

And he could see the shadows of more figures just out of reach, in back of them both, just inside the doorway, and beyond the neighbour's fence-top; and he realised then that he'd be up against this whole new gang of interbred lunatics, bent on honour because of her newly hustled name.

As the man moved to enter the yard, Cladan bounced him back with the wire gate, and he stumbled backwards on his heels across the narrow path, clambering between parked cars, and as he fell out onto the road, a screeching cab ricocheted him through the air, head first into the windscreen of an oncoming van.

But that's not what the court heard.

Everyone there that night — including his wife — unanimously swore Cladan threw him into the traffic.

After his first year inside, Cladan would kill another man in self-defence — who'd lunge at him with a shiv, swearing to match his kidney scar on the other side — all of which compounded his stretch in jail by almost twice the time.

PART THREE

CURSE BY DECREE

By way of an uncommon act of sarcasm, Fintonia once sent Cladan flowers inside. But now they're old and withered like her words. If he had a skink — like old mad Ganga next door — he'd slip it in his ear, just so the scales might help rub out all her old paeans of love.

The moon might well be just a mirror, but she's still his complete world. In his mind, he can fully see her outside now: armed to the teeth, with a crank in each hand, and still his heart in her guts, grinding him out in the greenest of slivers. He wouldn't mind if he still didn't love her, but she cares for nothing. He knows it now. And people spit on him. What is he now, but some lemon the world only cares to bottle away? Deep down, he knows the rigmarole: he's a lost gamble of the heart; love's reeking refuse. Or *"damaged goods"* like she said. He cashed in her slip, and then she sold his bare toes. He'd walked along the line of love for a time, but part of it dangled into the water, and not even the toadies gave it notice. He knows now that's when he should've realised it was all a washout in the end, and doubled back when he still had the chance.

There are no friends inside. Just flustered dupes, kissing chains, sucking ropes. Each man curled up in his cell like a viper wrapped in leaves, camouflaged by unforgiven sin, those fucking cocoons. But everyone inside is in love. They love a brick, a speck of sand, a slash of mortar. Eating in their boxes, they glare dead at the wood, watching their old tattered memories winding through the same old mangled grains again. Everyone in lost trepidation of his wishes. Meat, a dream to the most unsavoury man. Blood, a dress everyone wears. Cladan's seen them all sinking pins in their eyes, running blades up their wasted arms. It all soon turns back the same: everyone crying in their mind till it seeps out their ears, with no one to ever help redeem them all. The guards only laugh down from the towers.

One day a flock of screeching cockatoos swooped down into the pound. They were immediately shot at from all sides, and soon all the guards were prancing about with iridescent crests tucked in their caps like they were guards of the Vatican. The warden filled his pillows with all the fluffy tufts and feathers. And one poor slump in his cell hung himself from all the tied twinings of their talons.

They all still freely rape and murder inside, just like they did when they were out. They open a few up here and there to see what's inside, just for something to do. There's raffles for the effect of crimson. Some bet for red. Some bet for purple. Some bet for the sweet memory of a loganberry pie.

A fist always finds its every matched face in the night. Always, some quick knee slunking someone down in a corner somewhere. Lips whisper along the drains after suppertime, and wishes fish a catch here and there; but they're always just minnows, pissing all over the place in thorough panic at the crunch. The last doors snap at night like traps; sealing cells like dust. Each moment plucked like a daisy done. The floors forever iced from the same old spilled inner hail.

Sometimes Cladan prays the world will end *"from all them fat bombs,"* as he rubs his groin into the concaves of the grout, lonely lapping his tongue along the lip of the slab.

He's watched the light globe swinging all night long, seeing nothing but moons in the day, suns in the night, breasts in the twilight as the fog drifts by the bars.

Inside, he's fucked and sucked and had the same. It's been seven gigantic years since the scent of a woman. They've got pics of them up on the walls of every cell, but after a while it just numbs their life. Like the old lifer Cas slowly strums on his ukulele with a busted thumb...

> *"Paper mache courtesans*
> *on the cooler walls,*
> *trash my weary trapezoid*
> *with every crescent fall."*

Mirror sex is a magic wallet inside. It gets him into a room, into a scene for pills — up the conk, behind the knees, shot deep into the old lonely eyeballs.

Sometimes solitude is the only peace for all. Sometimes, after the door is bolted, one can only be free.

Out in the corridors, mocking tongues at the screws wag through the locks in the cell doors. Most are whitewashed. A few are bashed up and down with truncheons till they're swollen and can't be sucked back in: each poor dupe stuck standing on the other side of the door in his cell, hooked up to the lock for hours, waiting for yet another lump to subside.

The moment Cladan falls asleep, the minute he begins to dream, a thief sneaks in and takes it, and he wakes up gasping empty.

Some nights he stands below the bars of his window, looking up at the sky, biting the crescent of a thumbnail off, and he holds it up high amongst the stars, clothing the moon, keeping his hand there steady for hours, dreaming homesick all night long, amazed at how it always matches to a tee.

The irony of it all, he sadly ponders — *an edge of myself and an empty world.*

But then up comes dawn to kick-start another missed beginning again, and he flicks it away, riddled with the stink of yet another lost day gone. His toenails don't work: it all crumbles away in broken flakes like dandruff. Sometimes he wishes he was a monkey.

It's French inside too. Each night hefty snails slime up the walls from the pound and sneak inside the cells to get out of range of all the bats' incessant radars. Like everyone else, Cladan patiently waits for each one to slowly come through the bars one by one, and then he shells them quick, roasts them up tight with a match, and chomps them down. Over several months he once collected so many homes, he filled his pillowcase with them all to use as a beanbag. Though he doesn't always eat them straight away. He likes to play with their antennae for a while, watching them bob in and out, and then he just touches them, and they bob back in again. He does this for hours. He usually has to wait a few minutes, because they think he'll get bored and give up, but he never gives up and is never bored. Mad Ganga burns their antennae off with a cigarette so they won't ever know where they're going again. Out in the pound, a whole scrum of cons will watch someone taunt a snail for days, watching it slowly getting lost, crashing out everywhere. It's the only time everyone ever laughs together, when someone really knows how to antagonize a snail. Softly talking down to it like a cop, reassuring everything's all right. Then, sure enough, the feelers succumb to the kindness they've all fallen for themselves, gently popping out in trust. Then in he goes with the blowtorch.

"*Now!*" they all scream. "*Right through to its slimy arse!*"

Often, it all ends wild when, out of the blue, someone jealous of all the focus suddenly snaps and squashes it with his boot. And if it's Ganga's beast, he just goes nuts, and one hell of a fight busts loose. And then it's lockdown again. At last.

No one writes to Cladan inside. No one ever did when he was out there anyway. He hasn't had a single visitor through all the years. He misses the beach, and driving along the Great Ocean Road with the window down and his elbow out in the sun, he dreams of about every triple minute. And a giant bed, with a tall bubbly woman, and a month of drinking, kissing and spooning is an eternal need inside for all.

Emotionally, Cladan knows he's done for. He knows there's no possible way he could ever transact that with anyone again.

Guilt still storms his mind when he lusts at himself on the loneliest of nights; though he fears more turning into everyone else inside, who've all goosed off so much over the years they have to use the hem of their shirts as lassoes because their carpels are completely shot. But everyone knows it always comes back. The drive returns. It's nature, he knows: a natural occurrence of crime in the eyes of the Lord. Food is the only importance. Weapons the only need. Knives in spines, the only currency. He's opened up his arse to an array of gangs, only because he's been threatened with a shiv to both of his kidneys now.

Some nights he's whipped with the skins of dolls. The guards wake him up, elbowing him in the back, robbing him of his pillow, and emptying its sack, then they flog him with the case, and as he screams half asleep, the crusted streaks of old teary dreams cut back into his face like knives, and they leave him there, bleeding, with a thousand butchered memories, laughing back down the corridor.

Cladan's wept so much that the tears that once long spat from his eyes now only dribble, and they tunnel down his cheeks into the crease of his nostrils where now a large rash about his nose peels and bursts. Sometimes they race too fast to settle in the rash and crash straight into his gob — his tongue instinctively lapping it all up.

The irony of it all, he often thinks — *filling up my mouth.*

Sometimes, whilst eating the daily gruel, he imagines he's eating his eyes, as if they've finally fallen with the tears, and he just keeps on chewing, hoping he won't ever have to see anything else again. Self-mutilation is a big sport inside, and contests won are usually surpassed. Sometimes he wishes he was killed. Killing, inside, is on everyone's mind. Some do it. Some get it. Some bet on it. Some just go on scratching.

At night, when they lock the door behind him, sometimes he kisses the hinges with his luck — that fucking gypsy rat.

47
DEATH'S TROUT

In the slow dying hour before dusk a lone wattlebird called out endlessly for a mate in the distance — its repertoire of tunes faintly pealing back through the bars of the window in Cladan's cell. Then someone shouted down the corridor: *"I'm gunna gut that bird! I'm gunna stuff it in a bag and burst it like a cloud!"*

Cladan was sprawled on his back with his hands behind his head, listening to it in tears as he stared off to one side where the sky had become a blotch on the wall. That call always reminded him of Flip Bay.

He'd just popped a fourth pill and his skin was still tingling from being stuck outside in the sun for the whole afternoon, where everyone just stood around whinging, and eyeing off each other's girlish behinds.

Scrawled on the wall beside him, amongst a tangle of old scribblings from years before, was one untouched giant phrase in shaded copperplate within a scroll: NO ONE EATS CAKE HERE.

Then a cell door slammed in the distance and the heavy lock being turned echoed like an old cannon being cocked down through the centuries. But after another silence fell, the bird no longer sang, or was gone.

Old blind Cas was just gutted the week before in his cell, and in everyone's minds they could all still hear his family wailing out in the car park over the wall, just waiting to get inside to see him for the whole day — bastard screws. He only had a week to go after 21 years. He used to wheeze on his harmonica at night and sing a bluesy song soon as the sun bottomed out across the valley...

"Somebody shot my little pig.
There's bacon all across my lawn.
Somebody shot my little hog.
An' boy, I just can't help but moan."

He'd always quip these old sayings all the time, like *"I know the world's been shaved by a drunken barber,"* and *"Temptation resisted is the true measure of character."*

And all he ever did was tell his funniest tales around the yards. His blindness never seemed to bother him though. In fact, he thought it was a real blast on not seeing any more ugliness again.

"Now, if God would only take my ears," he'd always say. (Whereas, a lot listening often wished He'd just take his tongue.)

He'd tell everyone out in the yard a particular poignant story of his life till everyone had heard it a dozen times and then he'd change tack and begin the rounds of another. One tale was about how he went down to Gunnamatta beach one summer. It was a boiling hot day and he sat down at the shore to listen for hours to the breaking of the surf. Crashing waves always sounded like applause to him: proof positive that the Creator first whipped up the world as just a kid, with all the self consciousness of youth imbued. But there was a real stink in the air, so he decided not to wade. (He had a fear of bacteria in those days and figured the coast was riddled with the stuff because of all the wild storms that'd slammed into Melbourne the week before.) Then he was suddenly nipped on the toe by a crab. At least that's what he was told it was, by some passing couple with lovey-dovey voices who saw it happen.

"It was a mistake," they shouted out to him. *"It must've thought you were a carcass!"*

He said he'd been *"Sitting there all day, enjoying the sun"* — blind as he was, with his giant sunglasses on — *"assuming the stench was of the sea."* Little did he know, until the strangers had told him, that the whole beach was littered with dead whales, and that he'd been sitting amongst them all for the whole day whilst enjoying the heat and the surf, *"never knowing a thing, though wondering of the incredible pong."*

For some reason this little scrape through life caught the whole block by surprise, and there was a laughter that was suddenly borne on the air that could not be tamed by the guards, and they had to open up the gates to let it go free to roam the world.

But Cas was gone now.

Cladan's cell was right across from his, and all of a sudden this overwhelming silence at night emerged and it rattled him. He missed their evening chats in the dark and all the tunes they shared over the years.

At night, he could always feel the evil everywhere around him. He could smell it in the old stone walls. It had a certain wet odor he could never stomach. It'd seep through everything like a summer sweat, dirtying up the place. He once wasted years trying to scrub it all down and stop it coming through. It always seemed to cloud his thoughts at night.

He sat up from his slab and leaned against the wall below the moonlight, swallowing the lump in his throat as the cheerless surroundings of order and emptiness ambushed his senses again — the cell bearing down on his childlike resentments. He remembered all the old years when his enemies were long asleep, already bored by hope; when laughter erupted in the tanks of his son's smile; when the sun was just an outlaw burning lucky on all the trees.

Out in the yard he's seen a thousand bitched souls only warmed by their infectious changing wishes. He's seen a million miles of men with the talk of courage become one long silent wall. It's all clear to him now, from the placid foetus to the innocent bystander — and every crooked bastard in between — everything is missing. Just the shrill of geese and mosquitoes stay with their intentions in this cryptic world.

But with stronger will, Cladan's basis of therapy still lies in the realised kiss. In a daze, he smacked at the world's lips, shore to shore, and asked for another dead future, as someone cackled out somewhere: *"On the news. The sex of Europe, cut out like a ram's!"*

Cladan turned on his little b/w set as he popped the last pill, but watched instead an expose on the peccadilloes of the current US president seeking re-election. But he was soon so out of it that the woman narrating started saying what he was dreaming as he stared at the screen in a daze and grew more and more stoned as the walls glistened with all the menace again ...

"The devil's gonads have been delivered to the White House. In a secret operating theatre, countless floors beneath the Oval Office, the president is being tested for inherent papal sympathies by the low aural administrations of 12-tone psalms — calmly proclaiming all the while that "Atonality is criminality" before the operation. To one side, on another table, the nurses apply that old hooked instrument to the First Lady, just to make sure that concurrently there are no stowaways before being fertilised. As she goes under, she

listens to the old Southern song that all First Ladies have ever surrendered to during such classified procedures:

> *'The sun is sunk,*
> *and the moon is mine,*
> *and all the stars*
> *are starring in your eyes.'*

Between both tables stands a giant 24 carat gold flag of the republic, caught in mid-flap of a vicious gale, just like that old tin rag Nixon left on the moon. The leader of the free world starts to slowly count backwards, thinking of his old civilian life as he loses consciousness. The chief surgeon begins to delicately cut into him, talking of an old Hank Fonda film, saying, "You could see Jane just trying to come out through his face." And a few nurses bantered about their favourite Fondas for a while, just to ease everyone's nerves a little as the Secret Service in masks and gowns watched on and listened. "Pay the bill, baby," murmured the secretary of state at the pump. "Power through national supernaturalism," sniggered an old cabinet stooge at the valves. The physicians heard them all, but paid no mind. Soon, the surgeon plucked a testicle from the president with tongs and dropped it into a stainless steel bowl — and they all listened to it roll around like a marble in a wok till it settled itself. The president groaned out loud and began to rave of several top secret memos he had read or been told about, they weren't sure. "There has so far been one million worlds. Four hundred emissaries arrive per day." Whilst on the sidelines the stenographers in gowns typed out everything he said. And then the First Lady drowsily responded from the table opposite: "I was so small as a tot my granny used me as her only napkin." Two of those exploring her insides, openly chuckled, as another cutter plucking the president's last ball, voiced heartily in a public tone: "As octogenarians, they will both duly hold hands. Unlike all the

others. Unsocialised. Unsexualised."
"Hear hear," everyone baahed in
unison, as if they were all back in
their stately chambers. Close by, the
carrier with the "football" flipped on
the radio issuing satellite news to all
stationed forces around the globe,
and they all quietened and listened
as the operation ensued with much
caution. The broadcaster spoke of
how various freedom fighters in one
land had been turning in their
munitions, and how in another,
conversely, they were forced to dig
their own graves with their teeth.
Then there was a report about
various drugs being developed by
brain biologists of the CIA, like
medicinal courage capsules for those
soldiers not too stupid and smitten
with tinges of conscience. "Chemicals
on goddamn legs!" one old general in
the viewing gallery seethed down
with rage. Then a silence fell again
as a nurse replaced fluid drips in the
folds of the president's elbows, and
they all peered in close to see how
they would attach the edges of

Lucifer's scrotum to fit the girlish groin of the leader of the free world. One agent listened at his tie phone: "I can hear breathing on the line." "It's probably goddamn God!" hissed the veep behind a surgical mask. On the other table the surgeons had just removed the rotted womb of the First Lady and were preparing to refashion it with a more durable material; it was all green and purple and black in odd patches, with great bleeding tumours, and heavily scarred from the many hasty abortions she'd secretly endured as an adolescent in the mountains. One quack voiced how it would make a grand tam o' shanter. But both tables were soon patching up. There was concern that the transplant would not work. It would take many months before they would know if they had been successful. To save face, as a cover for the president's absence to recuperate, the report issued publicly was that the president was receiving extensive medical treatment after his recent travels to the east, where he'd toured through filthy shanty towns as a means to upgrade his tough international image within the region and strap a little meat to his foreign policy. To account for his lengthy recovery, and to whip up a swell of patriotic sympathy, the rumour leaked to the nation was that the president had been poisoned a dozen times and had received the radiation of at least 100 chest x-rays and needed much time to healthily recuperate. Whilst in a secret wing of the Oval Office awaited a harem of beauties from every corner of the globe, ready to sate him of his deepest desires and duly sire, in the fullest majesty, the first battalion of Satan's patient army."

53
CROWD OF STRAW

There's a nest cuckoos fall from.
A hearth geckos climb to.
Up high amongst the leaves
Wishes whisper by
As curses fall slow.
Learn to fly...
Aim for strawwww...

Then a bird tumbles down, swooping wildly across the field as it unfolds, offering itself up to the baby blue.

But in the city the nest was an old tin cradle dangling outside the 20th floor of the Rialto building, and the gecko was coming up the lift with Cladan's pay. In his second year on parole Cladan was working there as a window washer, and living in a nearby rooming-house with a bunch of addicts and drunks. Then all of a sudden they took his squeegee away; retrenched him on the spot like he was nothing. He couldn't believe it as he slowly walked down Spencer Street in the heat, his feet clapping the path like a frogman inching to shore, unready for his first real submersion.

Who the hell will hire me now? he kept on wondering — *a mid-aged lag in rags?*

Sour mobs in black quickly shuffled to work everywhere, yawning their shiny faces off; lines of cars banking up for blocks. Cladan couldn't hear himself think with all the racket going on. Then as he passed a row of shops a tram slowly screeched by like nails down a blackboard, and a migraine popped between his eyes, and he tripped over his loose sole and fell sprawled on the path, staring up in a daze at everything around him: the traffic, the racket, all the scissor-feet and faces, people staring down at him with smirks as they passed.

He slowly sat up, feeling beaten by it all, and tried to laugh his way out of it, but the impulse suddenly abandoned him. He was just replaced by a machine after two dedicated years of performing grins. He felt like opening up his wrists and finally kissing it all goodbye, when a finch suddenly flew out of a store and perched on his shoulder, chirping its head off.

He looked to it with a squint — for fear of being pecked blind by its little axe — but it warbled happily in his face, with its claws clutched tight to his collar bone through his ratty shirt. Soon he was up on his feet again, as if it strangely lifted him, and it stayed with him as he slowly ambled around the corner and giggled up the hill towards home — and the bird was clearly whistling in his ear all the way.

Puffy-eyed office workers stared at him as he walked by, smiling wide as the footpath. He was hoping it'd stay with him long enough till he reached home, so he could show everyone from room to room. Then a baby magpie swooped down from behind and clipped it off his shoulder, and it tumbled over, snagging itself on his shirt, and lay upside-down on his chest, fluttering in a panic.

An instant wave of doom flooded his thoughts again as the wings beat hard against his chest. He wondered if it might be a sign he was about to have a heart attack and drop dead where he stood, and thought it just might be the way he'd go — his heart finally face to face with a bird in the end — like some karmic payback for the old gull he'd butchered for food all those years ago on the dunes when he was a kid.

But just as he reached for it, it freed itself and flew out of his hand and disappeared up into the sky as an old wino suddenly sidled up to him, announcing he was a swami.

"I want to help people relax!" he screamed, taking Cladan's last cigarette, with his crazy eyes spinning like a monkey's. Then he rushed off in a puff of smoke, in his flapping flares, with his thinning hair bobbing up and down like a chimney sweep.

Then another one yapped at him from behind, telling him how to cook eggplant.

"Don't strip it and fry it! Measure your pan! Pour in stock as thick as your thumb. Drop in 'nips, and trickle in cream. Imagine a pancake for Chrissakes! Don't touch the eggplant! Let it bake!" and he walked away, holding his rumbling guts like a rope as a steaming car crawled along the gutter with its thermostat wailing like a sax.

Cladan walked on, doubly dispirited — with his head pounding, and his eyes throbbing. The bird just gone only inflamed the original woe of just losing his job. He felt like he couldn't hook onto anything that even resembled a sliver of hope. Everything just kept getting snatched from him.

One block from home, he noticed a woman standing at a bus stop, and she was wearing a white summer dress just like his wife used to wear — the same frilly one she always threw on when they picked fruit up north to save for their home. He looked at her wistfully as he walked nearer, thinking of all the good times they'd had when they were first in love.

Then she scratched at her scalp like a cat and pulled a bug out of her hair and looked closely at it, then over at him with the same sneer as he passed, and stamped the wriggling thing dead. It reminded him of the exact same look of loathing an uppity screw coined *"Pivot"* used to give everyone inside, whenever he dropped a butt and ground it out with his toe.

"Pivot pivots," was the constant refrain from every con whenever he did it, and usually like bullfrogs, ricocheting all around the corridors, with everyone in fits — which soon drove him mad, till he quit and got out of the game altogether.

But just as a bus pulled up, the woman ransacked her purse for the fare, and suddenly Cladan was running down the street with it in his hand, and she was screaming blue murder after him.

But no one helped her. And no one stopped him. All the winos in the street just lounged about everywhere, and everyone in the bus just sat there with their eyes glued to every glass in a trance like each little window was their own TV ...

Under the shower the rough cake of soap dwindled down to a coin from filing off the morning's cold film of sweat till it was as thin as paper, and Cladan watched it sail down the plughole like a leaf down a drain.

"May God bless her and all who sail on her," he burbled underwater, like his ma once did that day launching the family lilo when he was a kid.

He leaned out of the window of his room, feeling clean as a berry, as night finally fell, burying a little of the day's relentless heat, but he left the light off as he guzzled on a bottle of beer in the dark and looked out at all the city lights around him. Water slowly dripped from his hair to his face, and fell down into the street, and he watched each drop disappear with a smile, hearing the Blue Danube blaring from someone's radio in another room.

He turned around and leant against the sill and pulled the roll of cash out of his pocket and recounted — there was $800 left after he'd just paid the rent. But soon as he felt bad about it, he turned back to the view and took a long swig, and shoved any concern to the back of his mind — lumped in the queue like everything else.

In the middle of the night, staggering drunk to the bog, Cladan spotted the old note still pinned to old Zolo's door down the hallway — STILL IN ST. VINNIE'S. Before he knew it, he threw a few things in a bag, snatched Zolo's car keys off the sideboard downstairs, and was suddenly zooming west out of town, shooting through Ballarat in a drunken blur, tapping his fingers through The Avenue of Trees, till he finally crossed the border into South Oz, where he took a room in the Adelaide Hills.

But it was even hotter there than back at home. A TV was on full blast two rooms away, and a couple was fighting upstairs. Cladan was sitting on a single bed — with an air con on the size of a fridge rattling above his head — and he swigged on a bottle of green ginger wine as he tried to write a letter to his wife, to finally get the last word in, no matter how many years had passed between them.

He scrawled out another page, getting drunker and angrier.

"What do you want from me? Blood?"

He thought about cutting himself open and splashing it all over the pages — to finger-paint his points. He tried the car keys against his fingertips, but they were too coarse. He wondered about getting something sharper for a while, but couldn't be bothered going back down to Zolo's car to rummage in the boot — thought he'd probably find a Stanley knife, or a machete, and make a real mess of himself. He thought about his arteries for a while and using the bottle top. But he didn't want to get tetanus. He didn't want to die. He just wanted to use his blood for a point to make: he wanted to go see his son. But he soon felt tired of it all, the whole thieving day — his job snatched away, then stealing the purse and the car, his whole stolen life in any case. So he shoved the letter aside and leant back on the bed, holding the bottle on his stomach, thinking about his stolen boy.

I wonder if he even remembers me, he thought — *I wonder how he wonders.*

When he woke in the dark early hour before dawn, with the lights still on, the air con rattling above him, he dozily grabbed at his things and staggered down the stairs to the silent country street and chugged off in cold stolen hops to the dawn...

The notion of a spine preoccupied Cladan's mind as he barreled down the unwavering stretch of the Nullarbor — that, and his sudden gumption to go chase up his blood. He drove on for what seemed an eternity along the endless deserted road, daydreaming all the way, napping at truck stops here and there. Then he drove on again for another long barren stretch in the dark.

Strange thoughts and the oddest memories were jostling for focus in his mind, and he shifted his head side to side to stay awake as insects waltzed into the headlights and tap-danced to death on the screens of his eyes — the years churning through him without control.

Then daylight crept above the line again, and he snapped out of his daze and lit a smoke, and chased the shadows of clouds on the road for something to do; watching an eagle gliding in a spiral, snagged in the pull of a thermal rise.

He roared up through barren fields and old bruised bush terrain, and down wasted plateaus and across empty plains, and when a rare opposing car passed by every few hours or so, the driver waved to him. He was more surprised when the second one did it. But the third one subtly lifted his spirits.

Must be some old highway custom to keep everyone buoyant, he thought — *and help snap out of the monotony and what it does to your thoughts.*

Then he got eager about it, and started waving first — but no one waved back to him, and he felt cheated about everything again, and berated the whole world at the top of his lungs for miles on end. But suddenly, just as he began to wallow, someone passed and waved at him again.

I'm right, he thought, trying to convince himself — *I do feel good.*

Finally, he pulled up at the last stop roadhouse in the middle of nowhere to fill up and get a drink. Then someone pulled out, heading the other way, and waved him down, shouting out of the window, *"Your radiator's leaking!"*

This was a complete shock to him. Were all those drivers waving out of solidarity, like he thought, or purely out of warning all along? Did he misread everyone?

Fuming, he tightened up a hose and drove on further, watching a rainbow disappear over the highway as night began to fall — and he cynically noted out loud to himself: *"The sun always sucks the rainbow back like spaghetti."*

Come dusk Cladan parked in an empty truck stop to sleep another night in the car. A giant storm seemed to be brewing, even though it was stifling hot, but he couldn't see a thing around him. Electricity was in the air, and the sky was smothered with purple clouds, and the humidity was relentless — making it even more awkward to sleep on the back seat. And what, with no one with him, and nothing else around, and no light from anywhere — not from the moon, or the stars, or even a headlight from miles away — and with the horizon stretched for forever every way he turned, and fading like a ghost fast, it all began to spook him.

In no time lightning suddenly chiseled the sky all around him, and it was so stark and bright, it looked like daylight was trying to squeeze back in through the cracks.

Cladan was drenched with sweat, gluing himself to the vinyl seat, and then thunder rumbled on and on like it was building up for an almighty clap. Soon he couldn't grasp the notion of sleep anymore, with lightning crashing in everywhere, and his brain spinning like a top.

All the galahs groaning on a long road sign soon sought shelter under his car, and yawped up their cries below him before the next thunder rolled — and when that roll drummed on, the earth shook so hard the car rattled itself down to the chassis.

Then the odd fat splinter of rain loudly smacked the car like a coin on ice. One gob suddenly winged the side mirror, and it pealed out sharp as a plucked harp — shooting the hair up on the back of his neck. It was like the universe was popping all its rivets and about to completely implode.

Then the tall magnified shadow of a wildflower danced eerily across the windscreen, and it looked like a dinosaur vomiting up the world.

Cladan feared he was going to die — the storm creating even greater storms inside his head. He blew his nose and lighting flashed. A simple sniff and thunder drummed. His stomach rumbled and then thunder exploded, and an ocean of rain suddenly hammered down hard on top of him like artillery. And it wouldn't stop.

But, in the blackness of the racket, Cladan tried to divert his fears by thinking about it all like the way he might have once pondered it as a kid — and he spoke out loud to himself against the relentless hail, in a feeble attempt to protect himself, as the lightning flashed across the glass and the car shook beneath the rumbles...

"If my guts rumbled, and thunder rumbled at the same time, is the earth just a big rumbling stomach? And if the earth is just a big rumbling stomach, what else is out in space? Does the universe burp at one end? Is everyone just in a big thing so far away? Are we all just stuck in the giant gizzards of someone? Are the oceans just the acids of its lining, to keep the body of the cosmos in check? Are we all really just enzymes to keep the whole thing afloat?"

Cladan mumbled on and on like this throughout the duration of the storm, till finally he made himself so microscopic in the chaos and the racket and the dark, and in the scheme of everything let loose at large, that he slowly drifted off to sleep, mulling over yet another letter to his wife he'd never send...

My Dear Fin Soup,
No need to suppose anymore.
I want you to know that now.
Our anniversary brought up
so many memories over the years
I didn't even think were still there.

I don't know how to deal with it all
so readily now.
Don't mean to hurt you telling you
this, but — I hide you from my mind
now, because of all that, just to
protect myself from all the hurt I had.
I've just clammed up now,
because I daren't trust you again.
I don't trust anyone now too well
anyway.
I'm torn up about it all, I admit.
Don't know what to say really.
Maybe I'm a little blinded by it.
It's just another reason why.
I'm sickened by it all.
I never wrote to you because of it.
("Shoulder on the other side
is to lean on,
if you feel the need,"
you're telling me now?)
There's been so much spite, I know,
but I want you to weigh it up now
— do you think we can salvage it?
Are you rolling your eyes?
Though I wonder now,
how it'd all work out.
Isn't it all weird enough?
I've thought much more about it

the last year or so. (You too?)
Would the word bizarre suffice?
Or, "Well, no one lives there anymore."
(The way you used to say it.)
That irony.
I just hope I'm not wrong, not you.
Right now, I'm rolling up to be
hanged or hugged by our prize.
Be the least surprised.
(A pair of black shoes at the end.)
Love,
Your Cladding.

Driving into the red dust of Kalgoorlie, Cladan sourly thought of the mean fiery eyes of his estranged wife all over again. Inside that dragon was once a pearl wrapped in twine. Her belly was once a screen for the liturgy of dreams he'd long whispered through. Between her arms and legs a din endured, and then out came tumbling their son. She was riddled with hate. But not his boy, Fort, who ran away just as soon as he could — like his pop did, barely after they'd even begun.

By the time Fort had left his teens he'd wandered aimlessly across the land for a time with the faint hope of finding somewhere serene to settle, till one fateful day at a country fair he met a young equestrian called Shoona. She was as pale as an almond; an ally to a peach. Her hair was as red as blood, and her eyes were like fob watches, big and round, and green as limes. Her body was a broad tree, a shelter to the most gentle of creatures.

Cladan could see the cavern in her soul where his son now boarded. On the ground by her well crawled bandicoots and snails.

Jesus, Cladan thought — standing at the back of the shack, staring at her through the torn flywire door — *she looks like Snow fucking White.*

Shoona was sitting in the kitchen, gently pruning a fig. She let Cladan into the warm and homely silence. A money spider was spinning a web across the way, and Cladan had to tilt his head to get past it. Flies were hanging in webs all over the dusty windows, and fresh hot bread was reeking from an old iron stove.

Cladan walked into the lounge as a small fire crackled at a newly turned log in the hearth, and there was his son, watching footy on TV — a smoke burning in one hand, a frosty beer in the other. But Fort looked up calmly, as if one day he'd wholly expected to see his pop standing before him again. He'd heard of the old story from his ma years ago about how his pop once dashed off to Mexico to find his kin, and in time expected he'd be afforded the same quest once his pop had been released from jail.

"*Wanna game of table-tennis?*" Fort blurted out, nervously scratching at a corner of his lips.

Cladan quickly nodded — terrified of smiling too much at him.

They both rushed out to the garage and scrambled for the bats — Cladan clawed for red, but got blue instead. Both of them were soon playing hard, not like the old cautious way they'd last tapped a ball around when Fort was a tot and could barely walk.

Shoona soon brought them out a snack — a jug of fresh beer, and hot home-made bread with melted butter, spread thickly with salmon and chives, and all of it sprinkled with a subtle even layer of pepper and onion-salt — and left them alone again.

They both devoured the food in silence like it was just any old lunch they'd ever had together, when really they'd never shared all that many. But they savoured it, and treated the occasion as if everything was normal, knowing they'd both been waiting all their lives for it to happen.

They played again and again in the quiet for a while, bashing the ball from end to end, loading each hit with an emotional charge, sending back untold messages with each return — the longings, the angst, the love and all the losses — both of them infusing the ball with each one's long unsaid say. In time, Cladan laughed, and then his son laughed. They both leaned on the table laughing, and fell on the floor laughing. Pretty soon, they were both under the table chasing the ball, and crying and crawling to each other like babes, and embracing and forgiving one another for all the lost years and opportunities.

Days later, Cladan started the long drive back home all the way to his wife, with the bold theme of reconciliation stuck in his head after all the years they'd been apart. He wasn't all that sure he was doing the right thing, but he felt like he'd made peace with himself, and could resume his life again as if all the years he'd been boxed up had never happened. But as he turned a bend and headed back into the heart of Kalgoorlie he found a massive crowd swarming the streets, caught up in a riot.

Shops and pubs were burning, and black clouds from all the fires were filling up the sky. Locals were screaming out there was something in the beer, and running around like madmen everywhere. No one seemed to know what was real anymore. Everyone was hallucinating, and some were leaping off the roofs of the buildings to their deaths, seeing the crowds as straw.

Others declared objects were beginning to move of their own accord, and wailed out like banshees, biting at each other's ears like chimps. A few tourists were trying to hang themselves from street-posts, and soon a cop was being garroted in the main street. Nothing seemed possible to stop the nightmare from unfolding. The looks on people's faces fell like putty, and then faded like gas into the clag smoke. No one knew what to do.

Some people openly prayed, then wept in overwhelming agonies. One woman in the distance was holding a makeshift sign above the crowd: I ATE FISH! Cladan spotted it, and scrambled out of the car, and weaved through all the fists to talk to her, and find out what she meant, because he'd just eaten fish as well. But when he reached her, he realised the sign actually said: I HATE FISH!

"She's just as poisoned as the rest," he mumbled to himself.

Then he stumbled in a pothole, and crashed into someone, and they both fell over on top of another couple already down. And as a crowd swept through, other people began to fall on top of them all. Soon, there was a pile of people growing high as a bonfire, and Cladan was stuck near the bottom, wheezing under the crush. He squinted up towards the twilight sky, gasping for air, and all he could see was a sea of crying faces towering above him, all their tears raining down on him.

Then suddenly, from up high near the moon, someone at the apex, in silhouette, with jutting ears like his pop, softly whispered down in a strangulated tone, *"I... love... you... "*

SWIMMING IN MOOLOOPIA
TILL JUNE

I t was a dull green dawn when Cladan woke on the floor and there she was, still sitting at the pane as a reminder. The blunted sun in the lifting fog looked like a dinner gong on the roof of the house they were watching. He stretched out, yawning loud and long.

"*Why oh-why oh-why ... "*

"Ssshhh," she shushed back down at him, staring out through the venetian blind — her blinks slowing.

Cladan muted the yawn as it continued, then sneered *"zounds"* to himself as he rolled his eyes at the end. *The junk they roll into a ball and flick back at you,* was his first thought of the day. But really, it was just an echo of the last thing he'd mulled over at midnight when he'd finally stepped away from her to lie down on the mat and snooze again.

"Did they put the bin out?" he softly asked, clutching at his growling stomach.

But she only scoffed back a grunt at him.

This new sleepy town they were lumped in was dubbed Mooloopia, and everyone seemed to be on edge. Cladan thought some hick revelations would soon unfold to explain it all; but then, those suspicions always welled in whatever locale they were sent to case. Each town always had some dumb kneecapped taboo no one could ever tap. Even the rickety dogs had a creepy stealth.

The first school bus of the day soon rolled by, and a deep hollow drone of a light plane lingered on as it passed overhead. Thinning traffic crawled by over the speed bump out front, as drowsy locals dallied on their way to work. But nothing flinched at the house opposite. Everything was the same as yesterday. The venetian blinds were still crimped shut, even though it was getting sunny out.

They both knew the whole clan were still bottled up inside. A faint light in a back room would flicker on at dusk and glint above the blinds in a corner for the whole night till it bled out the dawn. What Cladan and Y were hired to do there was still kept from them. Y said it felt like they were in a Monopoly game:

the street's name was one of those in the upper echelons of the grid before GO! where if you put up one measly hotel and someone lands, you scoop the till. She was just aching for the call to run.

Cladan nearly smiled, and then wondered — *Was that her idea of a joke? Maybe she's more ironic than she lets on.*

Then a text message blooped on his phone, telling them to remain out of sight.

"Whadda they think we've been doing the last dozen moons?" he blurted out loud, sharing the screen with her.

"Ssshhh," she shushed again, sitting back down, staring out.

Cladan was still learning: "cult-busting" wasn't all it was cracked up to be. Though one block away was the last functioning drive-in in the state, so they'd pull their chairs up to the window each night as they eyed the house opposite and take in a movie as well.

Y was still hunched there — 13 nights in a row. Sometimes they'd fill in for the actors' voices and make up lines for a while for something to do. Sometimes they'd really ham it up, and it soon helped pass the time. But there was only so much Cladan could take in the end. Y never seemed to tire of it all though. She studied them religiously. Whereas Cladan thought it all wore a bit thin after a while and soon went back to the mat to nap whilst she kept rambling on in different voices. Though he never found any of it funny, and he noticed she was starting to cultivate a distinct, melodramatic tone that would, in odd ways, somehow find a knack at resurfacing when screaming at him later on.

But it was all business in the end, and that was the one thing Cladan respected about her — she never made jokes. It was like it was the one thing she could still hold back from him, just to keep a little part of herself for herself while stuck alone with him day and night. Whereas Cladan thought he was full of the stuff, and made every attempt, but still wasn't funny. He never made her laugh once, as long as he'd worked with her, and she was exactly the same. So he'd just try to sleep. And when it was her turn, she'd do the same. But Y only had a fortnight to stop the rot now and shut them down across the road, and she was in no mood for games anymore. Even though the changes made were late, neither of them could even begin to know what was in store for them there.

Y still wouldn't tell Cladan her name, no matter how much he pestered her.

All she ever snarled back was *"Why?"* when he first asked her, so he started parroting her that, years ago, and still asked her sometimes for fun, just to hear the way she'd say it. He had the notion that he truly knew her though. They used to mate like rabbits to wile the hours away in the early days, but that was long ago, when they first met. Now, they just sit back in the dark, peering through the blinds like a couple of old prunes in their rocking chairs waiting for the end. Though Cladan still had feelings for her — what those exactly were nowadays he wasn't sure of anymore. One thing that always tickled him about her was the way she'd suddenly blurt *"misery"* out of the blue, like she was straight out of some old Hollywood B movie on poverty row. He'd never heard that word out of a real live mouth before — but then she always was a bit of a movie case. Cladan used to slip dead matches back in the box, and when she'd step into the closet to light up a nail, all he'd ever hear was her striking them dumb and her muffled cries of *"misery"*...

Cladan sat down at the pane and stared down the house opposite as Y curled up into a ball on the mat and napped out for a while. He couldn't deny it to himself anymore — this tag team way of existing was beginning to rile him. It was only ever the fleeting sunshine that kept him afloat as always. He quickly devoured what was left of all the bite-size Cherry Ripes.

After a short power nap Y suddenly rose, opening up their work bag, and she lifted out the garden shears, and snipped them in the air near his face, with a smirk — much to his surprise, which strangely lifted him — and she headed out the front door to trim a hedge. It was only then, for the first time in days, that Cladan felt less troubled about everything.

It was a sunny morning, but still a little foggy out, and in odd patches the road seemed to gleam as gold. Cladan loved to watch her snip away. She had a subtle penchant for shapes, and the need to mend. And although she only did it to beef up the disguise of a genuine all-round suburban wife with greening thumbs — as a foil to keep a closer eye on the quarters opposite — she did it more for herself, for she was a country girl at heart and always craved the open air.

But what Cladan admired most about her was the way she could so openly satisfy her earthy whims whilst remaining perfectly attuned to the central task at hand.

Professionalism, he thought — staring out through the blind, as he reached over to the stand and wheeled the binoculars to his eyes.

On time, the postman soon pedaled to a stop and slipped the dummy letters in the box as expected — sent courtesy of their employ. Then Y went into her routine, and Cladan watched her in close up, like the way she always watched the screen above the roofs at night.

It's all a show, he mused. *The days, the nights...*

Dropping the shears, Y flipped back the box and removed a dozen letters, then turned to go back inside as she flicked through them. But as she subtly slipped a letter from inside her shirt to the pile, she suddenly stopped in her tracks — as if discovering one wrongly addressed — and looked vaguely about at the houses opposite, then crossed the road to the one in question and knocked on the front door, just to see who exactly would open up to her.

Cladan marveled at watching her deliver it, and focused in close to see the way she walked up the pathway in character, knowing just how much she was loving it. The subtle way she played the good wifely gardener and the comely Samaritan neighbour was a real tonic to him. He could see she had a real talent for the boards and sometimes wondered if she'd ever graced the stage when she was young.

The woman's gifted, he thought — refocusing. *She's got a flip Lillian Gish ... Karen Black thing going on.*

But no one answered the door. They were all still definitely home. They both knew that, without doubt. But no one budged an inch inside. So she slipped the envelope halfway under the door and crossed the road and headed back to the garden to resume her pruning. It was only then that the blind of the corner window opened to a slit, to take a peep, and closed again. Cladan and Y never really expected any of them to answer the door, but they knew they always took a slight gamble with the blinds. Y soon came back inside again.

"Corner blind blinked," Cladan said, staring through the binoculars, *"but no minces."*

"Watch the letter," she barked. *"I want the time."*

Y liked to play the conscience every now and again to keep herself primed for what might soon follow. But Cladan knew that was her forte, and he was fine with that. It was the specialty she was lumped with. And even though he found it tiring at times, catching all the run off, he understood it was simply a matter of exercise. Chances are, had she not kept herself tuned that way and hauled him in on a life buoy, he'd still be the derelict he once was, and not all that long ago. In his heart of hearts he's glad to have found a calling. The fact that it's not all gravy, and part and parcel of it is to be the whipping boy at times, is really of no consequence to him anymore. There was a time he long played the part, and was often the better for it. It got him through jail and he survived everything thrown at him there. Sometimes he wonders though if there might be something more substantially drawn from within that he'll have to outlay to pay for it all. Still some slippery personal tax involved. He just wishes he knew what exactly this levy might be. He's always been a little touchy with transactions, let alone of the intangible kind, and of that imbalance — whatever the lump sum being extracted might be — slightly alarms him. The sheer notion of being somehow further debited — after all the years of being boxed up like a worm in Hell — seemed to broach all those set tenets of his creed that he's stubbornly returned to since his fluky rescue. The truth is, at bottom, he knew his faith was flawed, and he felt like all that that had long been heralded for all time had now fizzled; and he felt the distinct sensation that he may have in fact been burgled. But he sat glued to the spot and duly watched the letter for the rest of the afternoon, and waited for the final text to roll in.

As the first stars appeared all the white ghostly bugs came out in the twilight and settled themselves across the dusty panes in small collective swarms that resembled the hung pelts of weasels. Cladan and Y felt queasy with all of them writhing about everywhere under glass. They must've sprayed a dozen times in the window cracks before the streetlights flickered on, where they all finally fled to, and remained, orbiting up high with all the moths. Cladan briefly caught sight of the glassy rainbow wings of a cicada glistening in the moonlight as it clung to a tree in the front yard and sang its song. It reminded him of all those he'd witnessed for years at the back of the family store when he was a kid. It was the first one he'd seen since then, and when it darted off he wondered where its old crunchy shell might still hang. He made a mental note to check the back door in the morning.

Y was soon watching another tale unfurl across the stars, and Cladan just sat there with his not-so-secret flask, naval gazing as usual; forever stuck pondering over the same old crippled way each plan ever hatched had brought him to where he was again; chewing over and over the endless limbo of his wastrel life. He suddenly thought of the strange demise of his old chain-smoking cellmate, *"Torch"*, who ironically ended his span by self-combustion, leaving nothing but his knobbly pins in socks and sandals on the pedals of his rusty Beetle. Cladan read about his odd demise in the local rag and recalled how Torch had always wanted to be a quack in his youth, but only wound up a fixer of strays at the city pound before he started casing banks. After they were both released from jail they'd sometimes catch up for a beer and play bezique in a park between the city zoo and the state asylum, where they'd laugh it up drunk watching all the apes screeching at all those *"nuts"* across the road.

Y was again lost to the dirge flickering across the sky; her eyes glued to every move through the binoculars; her hands twitching with every blow. There was a multitude jujitsuing their way through a town, falling from the trees, spinning their stars everywhere they ran. Cladan looked over at her sitting in silhouette in the moonlight. She was just dying to act it all out again.

Would this be us in the end, our last deadly moves? he wondered, feeling suddenly uneasy again.

He looked at her thin slender hands sprung like coils.

How many dud cudded wishes have I burped on, he thought, *to just feel those at my hacking hips again?*

But Y soon took leave to water the tub, and Cladan was left alone again. Above the distant roofs were the green glowing letters of *INTERVAL*...

In the near distance a cat or a fox shrieked out in the darkness — Cladan wasn't sure. Then a doubled-up truck geared down as it rumbled past over the speed hump out front, rattling all the windows throughout the empty house. Cladan often wondered why Y was so headstrong, yet so insufferably obedient and punctual with everything she did. That robotic way of operating never more bothered him as it did then. He suddenly felt despondent about the whole thing they were there for anyway.

But then again, when she returned, didn't he end up stepping in the closet to light a nail, as if duly pushed to a break as her? Wasn't he doing exactly as she was, and simply refreshing himself as instructed? Wasn't he in there on account of being commanded, just as she surely was? The whole deep vein thrombosis scare was spooking everyone. Cladan was convinced he'd end up losing his pins. In the darkness of the closet he sourly mulled over all those old butchered ideals of love whispering in the back of his brain again.

The same old address, he thought — puffing away in yet another hole.

He thought of how the last few years he'd spent fraying his nerves at the panes of a dozen other hollow homes the same way, and how many plugholes she'd aimed her filthy water. It all suddenly seemed clear to him — it was not the proper way to pass. It still irked him, the lack of contact between them now; that old fire still burning below his guts for all time. He slyly guzzled on his flask in the dark as he listened out for her, and then bent his knees up and down for a while as he lit a second nail in the gloom.

What lost chances ever well, for each spent plea forever mulled? he loosely rambled in his mind, nearly blubbering, feeling a fool, as he walked on the spot in the dark like a marching loon.

He knew in the early days Y used to wonder about their bond the same way, and how they'd both suddenly changed and steered clear of one another like that. For a while he bluffed himself about it all and let it go. But now, with hindsight, he realised he'd always pretended his feelings then were really of lesser import; when in all truth, deep down, he knew they were just as strong as they'd ever been whenever they worked as a team together. But she'd only ever stand to duty now, and never entreat him to her passions again.

They soon both sat back at the pane and did as usual what was expected of them. It was all a routine. But, after a while, as the night wore on, they could each sense something was anew in the air. It was like a presence, as if someone else was in the house with them. Normally, nothing would rattle them, but now even the slightest annoyance — like the way each of them ate, or the way they spoke to one another — upset them profusely, regardless of more offending habits. But, by way of the old discipline long drilled into them, they soon knuckled down to their intentions, knowing fully well it was simply a matter of diligence to attain some sense of equilibrium again. Though, as midnight passed, they each privately felt tainted by even more strange and unfathomable concerns. As a fallback they each pondered over all those old romantic notions they once ritually took to as lovers. But after a while they suddenly felt that all those loose ends of their lives that had once bonded them were now frayed again; as if they weren't only torn from one another, but from within themselves, as if nothing had ever changed from the way they were before, before they'd ever met each other.

They'd both called out love as just another crutch all along anyway. They were both wholly resigned to it wearing off as it did. Everything else was just a bonus anyway, after the strange empty lives on the streets they'd each led for so long. It was how they found one another — up to their guts in muck, and easy for the picking. The same old tale their lives had ever been. At heart each job was just another ticket to pass the time, another ride. But they soon felt even stranger than they did before, as if they really weren't alone at all. The odd lingering presence felt even more potent, and in a more collective plural sense, like a crowd was there — of many other presences — but neither of them could seem to mention it to one another.

Cladan thought over all the times they never knew the deed they were employed to conjure, right up till the last minute, and how they'd always acquiesced to whatever demand was asked of them. But now they felt uneasy, trying to stifle away little whispered arguments in their heads, and doubting all the while the voices were their own. The moon was like a spotlight. It was madness, they knew ...

The quietness of the night fell even deeper, and more sonorous, than they thought possible. Colourful slides of fanciful furs, and stacked steaming tacos, were already being slipped across the screen in the sky. Out of the blue, Y suddenly made a startlingly unprofessional move and boldly slipped out the back door and took a stroll the long way round there, through the back lanes, and soon brought back two sodden buckets of steaming corn, and they both just sat again at the pane in the dark and stuffed themselves, watching some crazed ghoul do its worst.

"More torsos and sauce," Cladan wheezed, bored with it all — trying to hide the fact he was already half-soused.

He looked back through the binoculars at the house opposite. They were all still boxed up inside, but they'd ceased using the light in back anymore, and it was too dark to see if the letter was gone. He wheeled the binoculars away, but Y grabbed the strap and pulled it back towards her eyes and watched the movie, starting up her voices again.

"I can't shoot that for shit, Sherlock!"

But Cladan wouldn't bite.

"This world's a bad apple. So clock me."

He was too busy looking around the empty room like he'd just missed something. Then he stared back at the shadows on the wall behind them, suspiciously looking for any sign of difference.

They both seemed wholly focused on being distracted. It was like nothing seemed to jell with them anymore. It was all soon clear to them that they'd neglected the house opposite. Hours had passed in their dereliction. Could they confidently say that all the others were still definitely boxed up inside anymore? They wondered out loud if perhaps the gang had picked up on their lapsed ways over the last few days and were now simply toying with them. Paranoia was rife between them. There was a time their steadfastness, and their vigilance, was their pride and joy. But now, they briefly speculated on just how sloppy they'd actually become. They each wondered why they felt more worse off than they could've ever imagined being.

Cladan subtly alluded to their mental health concerns, and asked Y if she felt okay; but Y said nothing more, and only stuffed handfuls of popcorn down her throat, with her eyes glued to the binoculars in a trance. She was in denial, and she knew it, but she just didn't seem to want to care anymore.

But the gas that welled within them as they gobbled down the starch! Both of them scuttling back to the closet to let them all go! They weren't above trumpeting in each other's faces — but the racket! The worst giveaway! And in greasy unison! So it was both back to the hole together, to choke on their own steam again, and light up their nails — though fearful one massive kaboom! was on the cards. Cladan openly pined for it. To the both of them it never seemed a worse sanctuary.

"This dumb fucking thumb holding us down," Cladan whined in the dark, puffing up again, and gassing it all away.

But Y said nothing, and only smoked, letting loose her own din as well, as she lifted her pins, shaking out her ankles in turn.

They were soon sitting back at the window again, and Y was licking her fingertips as she watched on. All that sickly puffed puke had bloated the both of them, and they just leaned back and again took a front seat to the chore, fatted with their own sudden apathy.

To really peacefully sleep on a job was often a dream that never played out all that well in the end. Sometimes they'd take turns after meals though, one at a time, with someone on the watch as the other blinked out for a spell. When finally Y did begin to snooze in her chair, it was always a fizzle each toke of air she snatched. But as she floundered, the menace in her seemed to leave. Occasionally, as she lightly slept, usually depending on how much she'd just gorged, she'd begin to purr like a lazing cat.

Has a definite motor problem, without question, Cladan thought — watching her subtly snore in the darkness for the thousandth time.

"Puddy, puddy," he whispered to her.

One night, in earlier times, purely as payback for barking orders at him night and day, Cladan squiggled a bush of black kitty whiskers across her cheeks with a felt pen as she slept, and she wore them about the safe house for days, never knowing a thing. Over time, he went on and on from there, adding tidbits each eve: fat dollar signs crossed over her eyes; long sabre fangs all the way down to her chin; a stupid eight ball on her nose like a dopey clown. She never knew about it as it faded over the final week there, but Cladan was always amazed at how stunning she still seemed.

Never could deface such a gem, he thought — *it clearly comes from within, not without and splashed on.*

The follow-up text never came through, and they knew they were running out of time. The weather had shifted again, and they could feel an inherent gloom closing in on them again. It was like the house was suddenly being squeezed on all sides and was about to pop its top like a boil. It started freaking them out. All those successfully staged ploys they'd carried out without qualms over the years as decoys, and now this — sheer and utter dilapidation.

It became apparent to them that they'd clearly failed; but mistakes were not to be tolerated, they fully knew. The record of their previous successes would never amount to much in the end. History was a bogus detail as far as their employ. It was merely a reference that enabled them to jump streams and continue on as hired guns in other ways.

They soon retreated from the pane to observe the goods from another angle — peering out from an empty bedroom at the far corner of the house — for the dreaded fear of their own well-being now took precedence. Even the closet seemed suddenly unsafe: their once and only unfailing sanctuary. They both knew that'd be the first cranny they'd sweep through if things turned ugly and came to a crunch.

But they couldn't comprehend why they hadn't gotten anywhere this time, or why they didn't even seem to regard their duties as earnestly as before. At first it all ran like clockwork. They did as they'd always done all those times before. It was second nature to them. They attended to all their chores, keeping one eye on their charges opposite, night and day. But they didn't understand what had happened this time, and they each wondered if maybe they were losing their bearings.

Were all those opposite still cooped up inside? None of them had stepped out for even a breath of fresh air, they were sure of it. They couldn't understand it all. Even their phones had stopped working. Maybe — they each privately pondered — there was something in the air, or the water, or the fickle climate.

Mooloopia? they wondered to themselves. *What does it mean?* They couldn't help but question everything.

It was a *"spiritual shutdown,"* Y seemed to sense, and reiterated the point again and again throughout the night, strangely panicked by all the quiet.

As for Cladan, she might as well have been speaking in tongues. He could only snatch at this and that she babbled on about, but overall it was still a complete riddle to him. He tried to rationalise what he could, in any feeble way he could manage, just to at least comprehend what little logic there was left to restore them back to the fray. They held no illusion to the fact that the odd atmosphere taking hold could be resolved anymore. They realised that all those old notions they'd each been bludgeoned with since they were kids were now just like childlike grasps at straw. Everything else seemed just a ruse. But the deterioration seemed clearly imminent to them. They could both feel it in tow. And they sensed it would all be over by the dawn. It seemed like there was no other possible outcome. It all suddenly seemed beyond them, what was about to unfold. They both knew they should've realised what would finally happen to them in the end, but they could never tickle their way clear of such intangible stakes for themselves. At first the idea of each of them suddenly unburdening themselves to one another gave them solace, and they confided in earnest their private truths, their secret longings, their personal shames, each and every crippling emotional quirk, but to no avail. In desperation, they soon confessed all on their knees to one another in the dark, and in tears begged above to the powers that be to be spared, and for all their efforts nothing changed but for the change itself.

They felt like it was inside them, and that it would never end, and that it would soon take its certain course to only bring on their comeuppance. It wasn't the notion of death they feared anymore. They both accepted they'd only fleetingly become and would just as fleetingly go. The transitory nature was not of immediate concern to them. The issue at hand seemed to be of a much more sacred note. It was as if something priceless within them had finally ripened, and was suddenly in the rapid stage of its decomposition. And they could feel that this rotting inside them was racing at an alarming rate. They could distinctly feel something deflowering within themselves, as if each and every ritualistic effort of old, long made to bring all back into grace, seemed to be of no import to them anymore. Each time the mere idea was exercised, it seemed as if another milestone had passed in the state of their own decay.

It seemed to go on and on, getting worse and worse in their minds, seeming only to worsen more with each breath they stole, and still it was clear to them there would be no salvation in the end. They felt like they would remain this way, worsening and worsening, without any conceivable lull or interim. They felt as if it would totally consume them, with not a chance of redemption in sight. It seemed like it would continue forever, and they felt like they were about to be everlastingly damned.

They both felt as physically healthy in flesh and blood as before, but something vast and unknowable seemed to be invading them, polluting all their nerves and emotions. It wasn't guilt or shame or regret or remorse. It was desertion. It was the end without end. It was more than that. It was the ousting of one's own established fortitude. It was sorrow in ambush. They felt like they were being bullied by their own inherent mystery. It was avowed retribution. Inert, they both felt. Frozen. Inert.

They both stared out the pane again in a daze, feeling strangely exhausted. No one was out in the street anymore. None of the old late night local dog walkers they first made fun of from behind the blind the first few nights they were perched there. A hard night had fallen, and it felt like all was further darkening.

Y suddenly turned away and didn't wish to look out anymore; sure that all they'd seen or heard had attuned them to their sudden downfall. But within minutes she immediately contradicted herself; suddenly sure it was simply a part of life all succumb to in the end. Illusions came and went, no matter how much they tried to resist or embrace them.

Then the river of the world came barreling down the road. It was a wide empyrean swell of unborn souls clamouring amongst themselves, and screaming in high anguished pitches the agonies of not being born. Its luminescence was blinding. Their deafening cries were of such varied strains that Cladan and Y were trembling, and their bodies seemed to be wracking from each and every harrowing cry of sorrow. They'd both lost all control of their bodily functions as the tortured wails bared down upon them and bored through their nerves like worms. A trillion screams plummeting deep within them. Organs at their sides — their livers, their spleens — were fluttering to the rhythm of the howls in ambush.

It was all rising outside. The choking tide of the world had come. It was seeping under the doors, wriggling about their heels like eels. The inundation was deafening; cries tearing at their hearts with anguish. They were both weeping uncontrollably, their endless tears blinding them, stinging them, burning up their cheeks, till soon their eyes were emptied and they could only cry out in dry-reaching retches.

Everything was pouring down their pins. They were letting go of everything, loosening their steady hold, unraveling themselves to the relentless calls of all. Y could no longer scream, no longer flay about in fear anymore.

She's dying, Cladan thought.

He thought he was dying as well.

Soon, he could no longer see her. It was all too bright, deafening and cold. Then, as the river topped the sills, the sky lightened.

"Is it twilight again?" Cladan rambled out loud. *"Is it day? Is the sun up? Is the moon out? Are they the stars? Is all this here for good?"*

They were both slipping away. It was all taking them along. It had dragged them away. The sky was there. Then it was all white again. Y had drifted away on her own.

The currents, the currents.

She was gone. They were both gone. All the darkness was gone, and all the light was gone. And all the cries were gone.

It was all over. It was all done. It was the clouds. It was the moon. It was the stars. It was the eyes. It was the blinding blood of ...